Secret of the Mountain Dog

Secret of the Mountain Dog

ELIZABETH CODY KIMMEL

Scholastic Press

NEW YORK

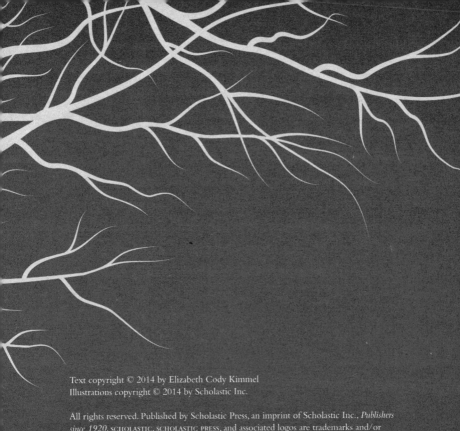

ISBN 978-0-545-74111-8
10 9 8 7 6 5 4 3 2 1   14 15 16 17 18
Printed in the U.S.A.   40
First printing, September 2014
The text type was set in Bembo.
The display type was set in Filth AOE.
Book design by Jeannine Riske

For Jackson Hummer,
the most mysterious reader I know.

Chapter One

It was in the middle of the road. Just sitting there, staring.

Staring at me.

For a moment, I thought it was a bear. There were plenty of bears roaming around the mountain, especially then, at the beginning of summer, when hibernation was a distant dream, and cubs were strong enough to accompany their mothers on the hunt. But as I stood paralyzed, my hand still reaching for the mailbox, I could see this wasn't a bear. It was a dog — the most enormous dog I had ever seen in my life.

His thick, abundant fur was a mix of red-gold and dark browns, and it stood up coarsely around his neck, like a lion's mane. He was tall even though seated, and he was built like a tank, thick and powerful. His eyes, firmly fixed on mine, were a deep hazel — familiar eyes that I felt I knew from somewhere, but I couldn't quite remember. What was he doing just sitting in the road like that?

Maybe he's hurt, I thought. But the dog didn't look hurt. He was sitting on his haunches, facing my driveway, his massive paws splayed on the hard-packed surface of the dirt road. Almost as though he'd been waiting for me.

I wanted to walk over to him, but I hesitated. It wasn't a good idea to approach a strange dog, especially one of this size. I had the distinction of being both the smallest and the fastest girl in my class in school, but even I couldn't sprint in flip-flops. Yet the more I looked at the dog, the more I wanted to pet him — to run my hands through that thick fur. He wasn't doing anything that seemed aggressive. But he wasn't doing anything overtly friendly, either.

As if he read my mind, the dog suddenly began wagging his tail, stirring up little clouds of dust from the dirt road. I took several steps toward him. The closer I got, the harder he wagged his tail. When I reached him, he lowered his head, which seemed to be his way of telling me not to worry — that I had nothing to fear from him.

When I touched his head, I couldn't believe how soft his fur was. It felt delicious and warm, like the sunlight itself.

"Hi," I said. "I'm Jax."

For some reason, it didn't feel stupid introducing myself to the dog. He lifted his head, gazed at me, then very gently nudged my hand with his nose.

"Are you lost?" I asked him. "I know you don't live in town — I would have noticed you. And we're the only house this far up the mountain. Where did you come from? Let's see if you have any tags."

I ran my hands through the fat mane of fur around his neck, but there was no collar. And yet he looked strong and healthy. His fur seemed neatly brushed, and his paws were perfectly clean. Dogs that got lost here on the mountain were likely to return home with burr-matted fur and mud-caked paws. This animal looked like he'd just stepped out of a pet salon.

"Do you want to come with me?" I asked. "So we can figure out where you belong?"

The dog stood up, still wagging his tail.

"Okay, then," I said. "Let's go."

I walked toward my house, the dog at my side. But when I got a few feet up the driveway, I realized he had stopped. I turned to look at him.

"Don't you want to come?" I asked.

He was standing next to the mailbox, tail still high, his bright eyes watching me. Then he glanced at the mailbox before returning his gaze to mine.

"Oh, I'm supposed to be getting the mail — thanks for reminding me," I said with a laugh.

Obviously, I was joking, though it's pretty weird to make a joke to a dog. But once I'd said it, it seemed he'd really done just that — stopped to remind me of the reason I'd walked down the driveway in the first place. As if he could not only understand my speech, but he could somehow understand what I was thinking. *Now, that's crazy — you've definitely been reading too many mysteries,* I told myself.

As I pulled a small bundle of letters and magazines from the mailbox, my eyes were drawn to a spot up high on the mountain where an old building sat all alone, like an abandoned fortress.

No one seemed to know who owned the building, or why it had been abandoned. It was only reachable by footpath, though at one time the old logging road had probably been passable too. I'd asked many people what the building was, and no one had a clue. I'd lived in Nolan all twelve years of my life and couldn't imagine wanting to live anywhere else in the world. I loved our little town nestled in the heart of the Catskill Mountains, where life was quiet and uncomplicated, and everyone knew everybody else. People around there often told stories about the empty building up on the mountain being haunted, that there were mysterious hidden rooms inside locked up tight, that a strange spectral figure had been glimpsed there — the usual haunted house stuff. Nothing you'd really take seriously.

I felt a sudden chill, although the sun was shining brightly and the air was already unseasonably warm for a June afternoon. I turned to look at the dog, who was watching me with patient intensity.

"Okay, boy, let's go," I said.

As we headed toward my house, the dog fell into step on my left side, as naturally as if we had been walking together every day for years. *He's obviously well trained,* I thought. *Somebody is definitely missing this dog right now.*

The front door of my house flew open with a bang, and a pink blur shot outside.

"What's his name? Does he like me? Can we keep him?"

"Kizzy, slow down! You can't run toward a dog like that — you'll scare him," I said. My sister's exuberance often irritated me, and today was no different.

But the dog appeared anything but scared. He walked right up to my sister and sat at her feet, his tail wagging. He looked over his shoulder at me and gave me a look that I found reassuring. Kizzy was a little small for five, and the dog almost reached her shoulder. He probably weighed four times what she did. Never one to be frightened of anything, Kizzy kneeled down and hugged him, burying her face in the thick fur around his neck. She practically disappeared into him — she looked like a blob of pink chewing gum stuck to his coat. I hoped Mom wouldn't get back from shopping and see Kizzy with a stray dog twice her size. She'd flip out. I walked around my sister and stuck my head in the front door.

"Dad?" I called. "Can you come outside for a minute?"

"Sure!" I heard him shout from upstairs. Moments later he appeared, book in hand, his black hair rumpled, and wearing a perplexed smile.

"Ah," he said, taking in the situation. "So Kizzy is a werewolf after all."

Kizzy extracted herself from the dog enough so that her face was showing.

"Am not," she declared. "Look what Jax found! He's very frenree — can we have him?"

"Boy, he is a beauty," Dad said, kneeling down next to Kizzy and stroking the dog's head. "Where did he come from?"

"He was just sitting in the road near the driveway," I said. "He doesn't have a collar or anything. I thought maybe we could try to find his owner."

My father nodded. "I could call the local vet, see if anyone's reported him missing. But they won't be open on a Sunday."

"Can he sleep over?" Kizzy asked, her eyes shining with excitement. My little sister could morph into a dangerously adorable creature when she wanted something, and right now she looked like she'd tumbled out of a Disney film. "Can he, Dad? Please?"

"He'd have to sleep outside — you know your mom isn't much of a dog-lover. Anyway, I don't even want to think about what would happen if he got anywhere near Whitman and Eliot," he added, chuckling.

Whitman and Eliot are our cats. They have a legendary hatred for dogs of all shapes and sizes. My aunt visits us every year, and once she made the mistake of bringing her miniature poodle with her. The cats took one look at him and pounced — they chased him all over the house, and by the time it was over, two lamps and a ceramic bowl were broken, and there were little puddles of poodle pee in every room.

"But he'll be cold if he has to sleep outside!" Kizzy cried, wrapping her arms around the dog again.

"No, he won't," I told her. "It's summertime. And with that coat of fur, Kiz, I doubt this dog would be cold even at the South Pole."

I heard the sound of gravel crunching under tires.

"Mom!" Kizzy shouted, leaping up and waving at the approaching car. "Don't worry, he's frenree! We're having a sleepover!"

Great. When was Kizzy going to figure out this wasn't the kind of news that was going to make our mother happy?

My mother gave us a confused half frown through the open window as she parked her old red Jeep by the garage. When she climbed out of the Jeep and got a better look at the dog, she froze.

"What is that doing here?" she asked, one hand still on the open Jeep door.

"Jax found him!" Kizzy announced triumphantly. "Look, he's ginormous!"

"You brought a stray dog to our house?" my mother asked, shaking her head with disbelief.

"He's not a stray — he's super healthy and well groomed," I said, trying to keep the irritation out of my voice. Anyone could see this dog wasn't a stray. "He's just lost. Dad said maybe we could kind of take care of him until the vet's office reopens tomorrow so we can find out if someone reported a lost dog."

I could see from her expression that she wasn't convinced. Why couldn't she just trust my judgment? "The vet will know how to find the owners," my father added. "I'm pretty sure this dog is a Tibetan mastiff — he looks like a purebred. Probably worth a small fortune. We'll have no trouble tracking down his family."

"Sleepover!" Kizzy cried, clapping. "Can he sleep with me?"

"Absolutely not!" my mother cried. "We don't know anything about this animal. He could have rabies, he could be vicious. He certainly can't go into the house. I mean it."

As if on cue, the dog stood up, brushed past my father, and trotted straight through the open front door.

"David, get him out of the house! Please!" my mother shouted in dismay.

"I wonder if he likes kitties," Kizzy mused softly.

"Uh-oh! I'll get him before the cats see him," my father said, going through the front door. Kizzy and I raced in behind him.

When Dad came to a sudden stop in the living room, we all collided, like in one of those old Marx Brothers movies on television. We peered around him to see what he was staring at.

"Now, that is odd," Dad said.

The dog was standing on the rug next to the couch. Less than a foot from his head, our orange tabby, Eliot, was curled up on the couch's arm. Eliot's eyes were half closed in his usual sleepy stupor. When the dog gave him a sniff, Eliot acted like he didn't notice. When he gave the cat a small lick on one ear, Eliot opened his mouth and yawned. Whitman came bounding into the room and stopped short when he caught sight of the dog. He arched his back and hissed.

This was the Whitman we knew and loved. Until he suddenly stopped acting like Whitman.

Whitman relaxed all at once — he went from arching and spitting to utter complacency in the space of one second, as if the dog had simply disappeared. The cat stretched luxuriously, drawing his coal-black legs out behind him and lengthening his spine. Then he casually walked right under the dog, appearing on the other side and pausing to lick his paw, like we'd always had a dog-shaped tunnel in the living room. Two cats that had always attacked any dog on sight seemed to have accepted this one without fanfare.

"He's magic," Kizzy said, her eyes wide with amazement.

I know that's something five-year-olds just say, but I couldn't help thinking the same thing. I'm twelve — I'll be a seventh grader when school starts again in the fall. Definitely too old to believe in magic. But nothing about this dog was ordinary. And now he was some kind of cat whisperer too?

"David?" my mother called from the doorway. "Did you catch it?"

Why did she have to refer to the dog as "it," as though he were a snake or a spider?

"He's right here, Karen," Dad replied. "Don't worry."

The dog wagged his tail and watched my father approach. Dad bent down and ran his hand through the fur around the dog's neck.

"Well, I thought there might be a collar hidden under all that fur, but there isn't," he said. "Come on, boy! Outside!"

The dog stared at my father, then abruptly lay down. I think, at that point, we probably all suspected this dog wasn't going to do anything he didn't want to do. And that included leaving our house.

"David, do something! He could take Kizzy's head off!"

My father took my mother's arm gently.

"Karen, this dog is obviously very healthy, and very tame," he said. "I really don't think there's any harm in letting him stay here while we find his owner. And I for one don't want to turn him loose on the mountain — that wouldn't be right. He can sleep in Jax's room with the door closed, so you won't have to worry about Kizzy."

I shot my father a grateful look, then kneeled next to the dog and hugged him. He smelled lightly of old wood and leaves.

"You can stay," I whispered. He lifted his head and looked at me with his beautiful gold-green eyes. Then he gave my hand a quick lick and rested his muzzle on my leg. No dog had ever acted like this around me. It was as if he'd chosen me. *I love him already!* I thought. *I totally and insanely love this dog.*

Mom was obviously not happy with the situation, but she went into the kitchen. Soon I could hear the sizzle of cooking food, and the smell of hamburgers filled the air. I spoke quietly to the dog, rubbing his ears and stroking his fur. He made a small sound of contentment in his throat and gazed up at me. He was so sweet! Whoever had lost him must be going crazy with worry. I imagined how thrilled his owners would be once we tracked them down, how grateful that we'd taken such good care of him. But the thought of someone driving away with him made me sad. I could probably go the rest of my life without ever finding another dog like this.

He behaved perfectly all through dinner, lying on the kitchen floor on a towel my dad put down for him, never begging for food or even eyeing our plates with pleading eyes the way some of my friends' dogs did. My mother didn't say much, and I could tell she was still unhappy about the dog. But Kizzy talked a mile a minute and spilled her lemonade twice, so there was plenty of noise. When we were finished eating, the dog continued to sit patiently while Dad put some leftover hamburger in a bowl and placed it on the floor. The food was gone in three gulps.

For the rest of the evening, the dog never left my side. He watched me wash the dishes, he curled up at my feet when I read in the living room, and at bedtime, he followed me into my room without even being called and installed himself near the foot of my bed.

"What do you say, boy?" I asked, inching down closer to him. He watched me with his startlingly clear eyes, then, as I began to scratch his ears, he rested his enormous head on my knee with a sigh.

"You like having your ears scratched, don't you?" I asked. He closed his eyes, and as I rubbed his soft ears, he made little two-syllable whines of contentment. It sounded like he was saying muh-muh.

"Muh-muh, huh?" I said. "Is that what you're saying? Mama? Or is it mo-mo?"

His eyes opened suddenly and his ears pricked up.

"Is that your name? Mo-Mo?"

His tail wagged enthusiastically.

"Okay, then, Mo-Mo," I said. "Now you know my name and I know yours. So we're officially friends. But I'm going to have to stop rubbing your ears for a minute so I can get my pajamas on."

Mo-Mo lifted his head, blinked once, then rolled onto his side.

I went into my bathroom, changed into the huge T-shirt I slept in, and brushed my teeth. On my way back to the bed, I switched the lights off and I was about to get under the covers when something outside caught my eye.

I walked over to my window and looked out. In the dim moonlight, I could see the vague outline of the old building on the mountain. As I watched it, I thought I saw a yellow-orange flicker. A moment later, I saw it again. Somebody was inside that building, someone who seemed to be moving past the windows with a flashlight. But those windows had been tightly boarded up for as long as I could remember.

I watched, holding my breath. I saw the light one more time, and then nothing. Who was it, and what were they doing up there in the middle of the night? I waited silently for a few minutes, but I saw no further signs of life.

When I turned back toward my bed, I exclaimed in surprise.

Mo-Mo was sitting up, rigid with attention, his ears pricked and his tail curled tight and still. He quivered slightly as he sat at full alert, watching intently. But it was not me that had his attention. Mo-Mo was looking past me. I turned and looked at the window behind me, then back at the dog.

Mo-Mo had seen the moving light too. Whatever was up there on the mountain had his attention. What kind of dog worried about lights up on the mountain where no lights should be? I felt a little shiver shoot up my spine, and I climbed into bed quickly, pulling the covers right up to my chin.

I did not look out the window again that night.

Chapter Two

The sun was a blazing rosy ball hanging low over the mountain when I opened my eyes. My clock radio said it was six thirty A.M. Weird. I almost never woke up this early unless an alarm went off. If neither of my parents knocked on my door, I'd been known to sleep through breakfast and lunch. But this morning, I felt wide awake and eager to get outside. I swung my feet onto the floor and almost shouted in surprise when I caught sight of the massive bulk of Mo-Mo sitting next to the door. I had forgotten about him.

"Hey, buddy," I said. "Do you need to go outside? Just give me a second to get ready, and I'll take you."

Mo-Mo stared at me like a sphinx with his wide, intelligent eyes as I pulled on my jeans and a faded purple sweatshirt.

I opened my bedroom door and walked down the hall to the living room, Mo-Mo padding quietly beside me. The house was perfectly silent. Even Whitman and Eliot were still asleep, curled around each other on the old couch that served as their bed, playground, and scratching post. Eliot opened one eye as Mo-Mo passed him. I tensed for possible conflict, but Eliot stayed where he was, his pink tongue darting out once to dampen his nose.

My mother had recently imposed a whole series of rules on my outdoor activities. One of the new rules was that I was supposed to be out on the mountain only in good weather and in daylight, never when a storm was forecast, and never without getting permission first. But everyone was asleep, and I was eager to go. I would leave a note in the middle of the kitchen table where my mother would see it as soon as she got up.

Early, around 6:45. Gone for a walk with the dog.
Sky is clear! And yes, I have my cell.

"Okay, Mo-Mo, I'm ready. Let's go."

It was an absolutely gorgeous day. Every blade of grass seemed lit from within under the orange morning sun. The sky itself looked immense, and from mountain to horizon, the whole world seemed somehow more spacious than usual.

Mo-Mo lifted his nose and sniffed the air. Then, without warning, he bounded down the driveway.

"No, wait!" I called, running after him. Mo-Mo was headed for the road, and though we never had much traffic, our driveway was on a dangerous blind curve. "Mo-Mo!"

To my relief, he executed a perfect U-turn and began galloping back toward me. I was amazed that such a huge dog could move so quickly and gracefully. Mo-Mo slowed to a trot as he approached me, his ears up and his tail curled tightly over his back. Then he circled behind me and took up position at my right side. He stayed there, matching his pace to mine, and we kept walking.

When we left the driveway and turned onto the dirt road, Mo-Mo pointed his nose toward the mountain again, where I could see the small white smudge of the old building.

"There was someone up there last night," I said. "Which is really strange. The only way to get there is to hike up Lotus Trail. Why would someone do that in the dark?"

As I spoke, something else occurred to me. Lotus Trail crossed over the road just by our driveway. Whoever I had seen on the mountain last night had entered the trail here, by my house. I felt a little shiver of fear tickle my spine at the thought of a stranger moving silently past my house in the dark. As if reading my mind, Mo-Mo suddenly trotted several yards ahead of me and stopped at the old stone cairn that marked the entrance to the trail. He sat down and looked at me, his tail thumping in the dirt.

"I think you want to go up there and investigate," I murmured.

Well, why shouldn't we? I had hiked Lotus Trail myself plenty of times. Whoever had been poking around in the old building was probably gone. And besides, I had the biggest dog on the planet as my escort, and that made me feel especially brave. Mo-Mo was sitting very still, watching me.

"Okay, then, let's go up," I said. I saw a flash in the dog's eyes for a moment, a glimmer of something. Gratitude, or anticipation, as if I'd just shown him a ball or a big stick. As we moved steadily up the trail, I wasn't sure if I was walking him or he was walking me. The higher we moved up the mountain, the faster Mo-Mo walked. I was starting to think it had been his plan to get me to hike up Lotus Trail just after sunrise, to the place where the strange light had flickered in the night.

We hiked in silence for fifteen minutes or so. I was huffing a bit as we climbed the steepest section of trail, where the view up the mountain was hidden by red oak and balsam fir trees and the path grew narrow and rocky. Then we emerged onto open mountain, and maybe a hundred yards off the trail lay the old empty building.

It looked more or less as I remembered it, an unremarkable rectangle of whitewashed walls with peeling maroon trim under a flat roof. But something was different. I frowned at the building, trying to work it out, and then it struck me. I could actually see a path to the building — where the way was usually overgrown and cluttered with brush. Someone had gone to a great deal of trouble to clear away all the brush, and it looked like it had been done very recently. Also, the windows were no longer boarded up.

It occurred to me that maybe I should take a picture of it to show my dad. I was pulling my cell phone from my back pocket when I heard a noise, a sound I had never heard before — a long, deep moan that chilled me to the bone. My phone dropped from my hand and I stumbled back a step.

Mo-Mo had heard the sound too. His ears pricked up as his huge head turned toward the building, where the noise came from. But the dog didn't look frightened, as I was. He seemed to be listening with his whole body, frozen in place as if he were hypnotized. I'm not easily spooked up on the mountain — I'd been hiking alone up here countless times before and considered it an extension of my own backyard — but the strange drone was utterly unearthly.

Mo-Mo began walking along the path toward the building, wagging his tail.

Was this where the dog had come from? Was the person who'd been up here last night Mo-Mo's owner? It was very possible. But I certainly wasn't going to leave him here without finding out for sure. The dog was my responsibility now, and I had to make sure he was safe. Grabbing my cell phone from where I had dropped it on the grass, I followed Mo-Mo. With each step I took, the strange keening grew louder.

When I reached the building, I realized the wall I could see from Lotus Trail was the structure's side, not its front. The path circled, and Mo-Mo was already rounding the corner, his tail slipping out of view. I followed him, but more cautiously now, unsure what I'd find. When I reached the corner, I took only a step or two beyond it. What I saw brought me to an immediate halt.

There was an old man in a maroon robe, sitting on the grass. His eyes were closed, his face deeply lined with age, his snow-white hair in a close-cropped crew cut. His spine was perfectly straight, his hands resting on his knees, and his expression peaceful. When he took a breath, there was a slight interruption in the droning sound, and I realized the noise was coming from him. Mo-Mo trotted to his side, plopped himself down on the grass, and appeared to fall immediately asleep as if he'd found an old friend.

Okay. So that seemed to solve the mystery of Mo-Mo. He obviously belonged with this man — he had gone straight to him. So I should just go, because I certainly wasn't going to interrupt him in the middle of . . . whatever it was that he was doing. But I couldn't bring myself to turn away. Not just yet. There was something so mysterious and captivating about the old man's face. Now that I realized the strange noise was actually something he was doing, it no longer seemed frightening. In fact, I didn't want to stop listening. I didn't want to take my eyes off the old man who sat in such perfect stillness, as if he belonged on that patch of grass and it could not exist without him.

"He's throat singing," came a voice from directly behind me.

I whirled around in surprise, and came face-to-face with a smiling boy who looked about my age. He was wearing jeans and a red T-shirt, and had glossy, jet-black hair and the same almond-brown skin as the old man.

"What?"

"Jampa-la," he said, pointing at the old man. "He's throat singing. Sometimes he calls it soul rattling."

I just stood there for a moment, with my mouth hanging open. I had ten questions I wanted to ask at once, but not one of them made it to my lips.

"I'm Yeshi," he said.

"Um, hi," I said. I looked over at the old man, who seemed to be completely unaware of our presence. "I'm Jackson. Everyone calls me Jax. Is . . . is that your grandfather?"

Yeshi shook his head.

"He's my teacher," he corrected. "But like a grandfather, maybe. Jampa Rinpoche is everyone's grandfather."

"Rin-po-shay?" I asked.

Yeshi nodded, and I noticed all at once that the sound of throat singing had stopped.

The old man, Jampa Rinpoche, was watching us. His eyes were bright and glittering, and a small smile played about his lips. He stood up and walked toward me. His long maroon robe, which he wore slung over one shoulder like a toga, brushed the grass with each step. Mo-Mo sprang to his feet and followed him.

"Rinpoche, this is Jax," Yeshi said.

Jampa Rinpoche smiled, deepening the wrinkles around his eyes and mouth. He pressed his palms together, making prayer hands.

"Tashi delek," he said.

"Tashee duh-lay," I repeated, hoping I was saying something like hello, and not "please leave this place now."

"Very good!" Yeshi said, looking delighted. "You are already speaking Tibetan, Jax."

"You're from Tibet?" I asked. Yeshi nodded.

Most everything I knew about the country I'd learned from my well-thumbed copy of *Tintin in Tibet*, possibly not the most credible source. I knew it was a country of snowcapped mountains and wild horses and Buddhist monks.

"Oh, you're a monk!" I exclaimed to Jampa, and instantly reddened with embarrassment.

But Jampa Rinpoche simply pressed his hands together again, then walked silently toward a door I had not noticed earlier. He opened it and disappeared into the building. Mo-Mo sat in the grass, watching but not following.

"I've never met a monk before," I said.

"How do you know?" asked Yeshi.

I was stumped by his question.

"I . . . well, you know. I would have noticed, I guess."

Yeshi shrugged. "Maybe. Maybe not. Not all monks look the same," he said. "Do you want me to show you around? Wait until you see the well! I can run a bucket down it and get all the fresh water I want!"

"Sure," I told him, wondering why he seemed so enthusiastic about fresh water. Was there no plumbing in the building? We walked together across the grass, past the spot where Jampa Rinpoche had been sitting. "So, Yeshi," I said, finally asking one of the many questions that was crowding my brain, "is this your house?"

"This is Tangyeling. It's a monastery."

"A monastery? But it's empty. It's always been empty. Everyone who lives around here says so."

Yeshi nodded. "Many years ago, Rinpoche traveled here to meet a wealthy American student. Together they built Tangyeling for Rinpoche's teacher so that he could come to America to live and take on new students. But

Rinpoche's teacher died in Tibet before ever seeing Tangyeling. Since then, for nearly thirty years, Rinpoche has been waiting."

I liked the way Yeshi talked, his accent not quite British, not quite Indian, but something musical in between the two. He grinned at me, and his dark brown eyes sparkled. I decided all at once that I liked him.

"What was Rinpoche waiting for?" I asked.

We stopped at a small circular wall of stones, topped with a lid of wood.

"For his teacher to come back," Yeshi said. "And now he has."

I stared at Yeshi in confusion as he pulled the wooden lid off of the stones.

"But you said his teacher died," I said.

"That's right. Look, the bucket hangs in here. I drop it down until I hear a splash, then pull it back up with the rope, and there is the water. Do you want to try?"

I took the handle of the bucket from Yeshi, leaned over the well, and let it drop. A second or so later, I heard it hit the water and began pulling it back up. It was harder than I thought. The bucket was heavy and kept swinging against the wall. It was only about half full when I got it to the surface.

"Try a drink," Yeshi urged.

I did. It was cold and pure and delicious. Much better than the stuff that came out of the tap at my house.

"That's the best water I've ever tasted," I said truthfully.

Yeshi beamed as if he were personally responsible for it.

"So you and Rinpoche are here to reopen the monastery for his teacher?" I asked. *The one who died?* I added silently.

"That's right," said Yeshi. "And also because there is something hidden here, something important, that Rinpoche says we must find."

"What kind of thing? Buried treasure?" I asked, half teasing.

Yeshi hung the bucket back on its hook and slid the wooden cover back onto the well. A worried frown creased his forehead as he turned and looked toward the monastery.

"A demon," he replied.

And at the very moment he said it, a cloud passed over the sun, and in the chill that followed, I heard Mo-Mo begin to howl.

Chapter Three

"What's wrong with him? Is he hurt?" Yeshi asked with concern as Mo-Mo continued his bizarre soft howling.

"I don't know. Has he ever done this before?" I asked.

Yeshi gave me a strange look.

"Why would I know?" he asked.

"Well, he's your dog, right?"

Yeshi shook his head, his eyes back on Mo-Mo.

"Rinpoche's dog, then," I pressed.

"No," Yeshi said. "I have never seen this dog until today."

The howling continued.

"Mo-Mo! It's okay! Come here, boy!" I called.

Mo-Mo stopped howling and trotted over to me. Or so I thought. When Mo-Mo sat down, it was at Yeshi's feet, not mine. Mo-Mo gazed up at the boy, panting slightly. I felt a pang of jealousy, but I was also curious. Mo-Mo acted as if he knew and trusted both Yeshi and Rinpoche, although they had never seen him before.

Yeshi reached down and stroked the dog's head.

"I asked because I've never seen him either, until yesterday. He just showed up at my driveway. I live a little farther down on the mountain," I explained, kneeling in the grass so I could pet Mo-Mo's back — my pathetic way of reminding Mo-Mo that I was the one who'd taken him in last night. To my delight, the dog swung his huge head toward me and snuffled me with his nose. "I took him to my house so I could try to find his owner. He's lost, poor guy."

"Why do you think he is lost?" Yeshi asked, sitting down in the grass next to me. Mo-Mo loomed over both of us even while sitting. Yeshi began scratching the dog's ears, and Mo-Mo let out his happy groaning *mo-mo* sound in response.

"Well, because he doesn't have a human with him, or anyone to take care of him," I explained.

"He has you," Yeshi said.

"Well, only because he found me yesterday, and I took him in," I said.

"So he isn't lost, then," Yeshi said, looking satisfied.

I didn't know how to argue with Yeshi's strange logic. And to be honest, I liked the idea that Mo-Mo wasn't lost anymore because he had happened to find me, someone who loved him and wanted to take him in.

"I guess," I said. "He seems to feel at home up here too. Sure is a beautiful place for a monastery."

"Isn't it?" Yeshi exclaimed, nodding his agreement. "Rinpoche and I are making mani stones for a wall, and we're going to put up prayer flags. And we're going to paint some of the inside of the monastery! I love to paint. You won't recognize this place when we're done with it!"

"Yeshi?" I asked. "What did you mean when you said there was a demon hidden here?"

Yeshi's hand froze over Mo-Mo's head mid-scratch. He sat back on the grass and looked at me for a long moment with his clear brown eyes. I had the feeling I was being evaluated in some way.

"You are good at keeping secrets," he said. He wasn't asking me, he was telling me. And he happened to be right. I'm not the kind of person who needs tons of friends — I prefer to have just one or two. But once I make a friend, I'm loyal for life.

"Yes, I am," I confirmed.

Yeshi nodded seriously.

"When Tangyeling was finished, and Rinpoche's teacher was set to come, important lamas and teachers from all over Tibet and India and Bhutan sent gifts. That is the custom. The boxes and crates were put in a storage room beneath the monastery so that they could be opened when Rinpoche's teacher arrived. But then he died. Tangyeling was locked up, and the boxes were never opened. Rinpoche believes the demon may be hidden somewhere in the monastery. I think it might be in one of those boxes."

"The demon's in a *box*?" I asked. The sun went behind a cloud again, and I shivered.

"A statue of it," Yeshi said. "Rinpoche knows, but he has not told me much about it. He says the statue is very powerful, and very dangerous. Whoever finds it must know the proper way to handle it, and the correct prayers to recite. The statue itself must have some means of calling or activating Tsiu Marpo."

"Zoomarpo?" I repeated.

Mo-Mo whimpered and looked from me to Yeshi with worried eyes.

Yeshi nodded, glancing over his shoulder at the monastery, as though he were afraid it could hear him. "That is the demon's name," he said quietly.

I felt the thrill of real, unfettered fear crackle up my spine.

"Who . . . what is he?"

"He is a protector of the teachings," Yeshi said. "He didn't start out that way. In ancient times, he was a terrible, wrathful demon. But a powerful master subdued him hundreds of years ago, and from that time on, he has been a protector demon for a monastery. But still a demon. Very dangerous."

"What does he look like?" I asked. The whole idea of a demon was extremely scary, but I figured at this point that I'd rather know than not know what the thing looked like.

Yeshi closed his eyes. They remained closed as he spoke.

"His skin is red, like fire, and his lips are frozen in a snarl. He wears silk robes of blue and red, and a coat covered with the shells of a thousand scorpions. On his head is a helmet lined with five silver skulls, and around his waist he wears a golden belt of jewels. He carries a spear in his right hand, and a lasso in his left, and he is riding a horse that is all black except its feet, which are white. When he rides, six demons ride with him. You will know he is coming by the sound of clattering hooves."

Okay. I was really wishing I *hadn't* asked now. I gulped audibly.

Yeshi opened his eyes and looked at me.

"He scares me too," he said quietly.

I didn't find that at all comforting.

"What will you do with the statue when you find it?" I asked.

"Rinpoche will know what to do," Yeshi assured me. "But to start with, he must bring it back to the monastery in Tibet, where it came from. It is very, very important that the statue be returned to its rightful home."

The whole thing was crazy, like something straight out of one of my Tintin books. As crazy as it sounded, I believed what Yeshi was telling me. There was something about him, something so clear and present, that made me feel I could trust him absolutely.

We sat in silence, Mo-Mo curled on the grass between us. The wind whispered through the trees, and high in the sky a hawk circled. I had probably been up this mountain a hundred times, but today it felt different, like a magical place that both belonged and did not belong in the real world. A place that managed to feel very safe and very dangerous at the same time.

My phone chimed and buzzed, startling me out of what I realized had become a prolonged daydream.

"That's my phone," I said to Yeshi. "Someone's texting me — probably my parents."

I held up my phone to show him.

"Texting is a way you can send messages on a phone that you can read on a screen," I explained.

Yeshi grinned. "I know that," he said. "We have cell phones in Tibet too."

My face reddened again. "Right," I said. "Sorry."

"That's okay. I've never seen one like yours, and I've never had one of my own, either."

I looked at the screen. The message was from my mother, asking why I was taking so long and if something was wrong. She wanted me to come home for lunch. I had no idea this much time had passed — it was almost ten o'clock.

"Uh-oh, I've been gone longer than I thought. My

mother worries a lot. She wants me to be home for lunch. I should probably go down soon."

I typed as I talked, sending a quick message that I was fine and had just lost track of the time.

"Okay," Yeshi said. "I have to help Rinpoche with chores. But this afternoon, he will sit for two hours in meditation. I'm going to go down into the storage room then to explore."

I didn't want to leave. I wanted to hear more about Tibet, and I wanted to see for myself what was in that storage room. I wanted to know more about Yeshi and why he was here. And where were his parents? There were so many things I wanted to ask him. And I hadn't even seen the inside of the monastery yet.

"Maybe your mother will let you come back this afternoon, and we can open the room together," Yeshi suggested, reading my mind once again.

"Oh, I'd like that!" I said eagerly. "I'm sure she'll let me. She just . . . she kind of worries a lot. I have to show up and let her see I'm okay, that I still have all ten fingers and toes and that I'm filled with nutritious food. I'm sure I can come back after that."

Yeshi looked pleased.

"Good," he said. "Rinpoche will begin meditating at two. He does every day at the same time. He will not need me for any chores during that time. Can you come then?"

"Definitely," I said, getting to my feet. Mo-Mo got up too. "Do you think there's a light down there, or should I bring a flashlight?"

"We don't have electricity yet, except for a little generator. There aren't any electric lights in the monastery anyway, and I have only one flashlight."

"Okay, I'll bring something," I said.

"Jax? I'm glad you found us," Yeshi said.

It was kind of a strange way to put it, but I was glad too.

"How long are you staying?" I asked.

Yeshi shrugged. "As long as it takes," he said. "We will have enough time. Maybe soon you can have dinner with us, and taste Rinpoche's rice and my momos."

"Mo-Mo's?" I asked, not daring to look at the dog.

"A momo is a Tibetan dumpling," Yeshi explained. "Very tasty."

I stood frozen for a moment, my mouth hanging open. Yeshi laughed. "You look like you want to eat one right now!"

I shook my head. "I'm just . . . it's only, I'm trying to figure it all out. I named the dog Mo-Mo because . . . I don't know, it just came to me because of this sound he was making. And he's a Tibetan mastiff. And then I run into you and Rinpoche, and *you're* Tibetan. And now you're telling me the name I randomly gave the dog is a Tibetan word too."

"That's right," Yeshi said.

"Okay, don't you find that sort of . . . unbelievable?"

"Well, it happened," Yeshi said simply. "Anyway, nothing is unbelievable when you come from Tibet."

Yeshi's words echoed in my head as I trudged down Lotus Trail, Mo-Mo at my heels. Nothing is unbelievable in Tibet.

Nothing is unbelievable.

Chapter Four

"I want to see the monkey!" Kizzy shouted, with peanut butter smeared on her lips as she squeezed her sandwich excitedly.

"Not a monkey, Kizz, a monk!" I said, laughing. "He's like a kind of priest, I guess. From Tibet."

"Where's Tibet?" Kizzy pressed.

"It's . . . uh . . . way far away. Near India," I added, which was just a guess on my part. I made a mental note to look it up later. I suddenly wanted to know everything I could about Tibet.

"I'm not sure I'm happy about any of this," my mother said, placing a glass of milk on the table in front of me. "I don't like the idea of some strange group starting up on the mountain."

A sound of irritation rose in my throat, but I quickly swallowed it. She'd been this way all year, suspicious of everything and everyone.

"It's not some strange group, Mom. It's just Yeshi and Rinpoche. They're Buddhists."

My mother pressed her lips together as she wiped imaginary crumbs off the table.

"Well, whoever they claim to be, we need to give them their privacy."

I froze with my hand halfway to my glass. Whoever they claim to be? I had just told her I'd met them both. That they were fine. But she obviously didn't believe me.

A year ago, I could have roamed the mountain to my heart's content with only casual concerns from my mother about my wearing enough sunblock and tick spray. But lately she had been refusing to give me the freedom I'd always enjoyed. She seemed to be afraid of virtually everything. Hardly a week went by without her announcing a new "rule." And there was no doubt in my mind about it — she was getting worse. If she made some unilateral decision that the monastery was off-limits, it was going to make the summer miserable for me. Yeshi and I were friends now. And I'd already decided to spend every possible moment with him since there was no way to know how long he was going to be staying. But of course, now my mother wanted to ruin that, so I'd have to spend the entire summer sitting in the house and doing nothing.

I chose my words very carefully.

"You're right, exactly. They're very quiet people. Hey, Mom, is there an apple or pear I can have for dessert?"

My mother's face brightened as it always did when I requested a fruit or a vegetable, which was not very often.

"How about a peach?" she asked, getting up and going over to the counter.

"Perfect," I said. "Oh, I need to find a couple of flashlights. I actually told Yeshi I'd bring them to him this afternoon. I think they've had an issue with their electricity, or something. The last thing we want is for one of them to take a fall in the dark, right?"

My mother handed me the peach silently. The frown on her face told me she was far from convinced.

"I can use those electric lanterns I got for camping, right?" I pressed. "The two Dad gave me, I mean. Would that be okay? I'd feel better knowing they were safe. It's like you always say, sometimes you don't know you need a flashlight until you fall over something and hurt yourself."

"Uh-oh," Kizzy said.

She had peeled open her sandwich and had run her fingers over the insides, creating a little food painting. Now a small chunk of jelly-tinged peanut butter was smeared into her hair.

"Oh, Cassandra, now you're going to have to have a bath so I can wash your hair," my mother exclaimed.

My mother was distracted with my little sister. I saw my chance and grabbed it.

"So is that okay, Mom?"

"I suppose," she replied, taking Kizzy's plate away.

"I want to bring the monkey a lantern too!" Kizzy protested.

"Sorry, kiddo. You've got to get hosed down, or better yet — put through a car wash!" I teased, standing up.

I rinsed my plate quickly and put it in the dishwasher, then left the kitchen before my mother could change her mind.

Mo-Mo was sitting patiently in my bedroom, where I'd left him, not wanting to antagonize my mother with the reminder of our enormous canine guest. I grabbed the two electric lanterns from my closet and tossed them in a backpack, along with an extra set of batteries and several granola bars.

It wasn't even one o'clock yet, and the hike up to the monastery took less than a half hour. Mo-Mo and I would get there early if we left now. But I didn't want to stick around the house. Once my mother's attention was no longer on Kizzy, she'd probably forbid me to go.

"Let's get moving, Mo-Mo," I said, slipping my arms through the straps of the backpack. "Back up the mountain."

We hiked Lotus Trail at a leisurely pace, with me stopping several times to examine flowers or snap a photograph with my phone. I was still twenty minutes early when Mo-Mo and I turned onto the monastery path.

There was no one in sight, though I could see signs of activity. Lines of little flags had been strung between the building and the trees nearest it. I walked over and lay down on the grass beneath the rows of fluttering colored cloth. The flags were arranged in a repeating series of blue, white, red, green, and yellow. As I stared up at them, I saw that each flag was covered in writing and squares of little illustrations. From my viewpoint in the grass, the lines of flags seemed to run right across the center of the sky.

With Mo-Mo stretched along my side, I grew increasingly relaxed, fascinated by the way each flag rippled and fluttered in the wind, making the words and the drawings appear to dance. I felt heavy, as if my body were pressing hard into the earth, or the earth pressing hard against me. At some point, I went from drowsy to actually sleeping. In my dream, I was exactly where I was, lying on the grass under rows of colorful flags on the mountain. But as I watched the flags, they turned into jewels — sapphires, rubies, and emeralds swept aloft by the wind and skating through the sky.

Then I felt something wet brush my ear, and I opened my eyes.

"Ha," Yeshi said. "You fell asleep. Mo-Mo was licking your ear and you didn't even move."

I sat up quickly, flushing with embarrassment at being caught sleeping. Did I snore? Did I drool? I didn't even want to know.

"You were only asleep for a minute," Yeshi said, smiling as he ran one hand through his mop of glossy black hair.

I was starting to get used to Yeshi talking as if he could hear what I was thinking. It should have felt creepy, but it didn't. I kind of liked it.

"I got hypnotized by the colors," I said.

"Prayer flags," Yeshi said. "We hung them today. Every time the wind blows, the prayers written on them are sent out to the world."

"They're beautiful. Um, I brought two electric lanterns," I told him, patting my backpack, then unzipping it. "And extra batteries just in case."

"These are great!" Yeshi said, pulling one of the lanterns out and switching it on, then off again. "Rinpoche is meditating now. So we can go down to the storeroom, but we will have to be very quiet."

I followed Yeshi over the grass to the monastery door, which I noticed had recently been painted the same maroon color as the trim below the roof. He opened the door, and in a little gallant gesture, he held it open for me. I paused for a fraction of a second. I was finally going to see the inside of the building that had been such a mystery for basically my whole life.

No one at school is going to believe this, I thought, then I almost laughed aloud at the thought. Dogs appearing out of nowhere, a monk throat singing on the mountain, a demon hidden in a monastery. No one at school was going to believe *any* of it.

I stepped over the threshold onto freshly swept hardwood floors. I was standing in a small alcove. On the wall facing me hung a large cloth painting of a blue Buddha surrounded by little balls of various colors. To the left was another maroon door, closed. And to my right, where Yeshi was pointing, was a hallway.

"Follow me," he whispered.

I noticed he had taken his shoes off, so I took mine off too and set them next to his on a little wooden rack by the doorway. We walked silently down the hallway to a door at the end, Mo-Mo padding quietly behind us. When Yeshi opened the door, I followed him into a brightly lit room. As soon as he closed the door, he spoke in his normal voice.

"Kitchen," he said, pointing at a neat little sink and stove by the window.

It was a cheerful, tidy room, with pretty little yellow curtains in both of the windows. A sturdy-looking wooden table with two old chairs sat near an alcove opening into another hall.

"Rinpoche and I have our bedrooms down that way," Yeshi said, nodding at the small hallway. "But this is where we want to go."

Yeshi walked over to another cloth painting, similar to the one I'd seen in the front hall, except that this

Buddha was not blue. Below the painting was a small table on which sat a copper-colored bowl, an orange, and a little bronze statue of a figure with many arms fanning up on either side like wings. Yeshi took down the Buddha painting, which I could now see was more like a wall hanging suspended from a single nail. Then he pushed the table aside, and I saw what had been a cleverly hidden little door. He reached into the pocket of his jeans and pulled out a large, old-fashioned key, which he slid into the keyhole. The door unlocked with a smooth click.

"I oiled it," Yeshi said, looking very pleased with himself. "Yesterday I could hardly get it open. Now it works like new. Nice and easy."

And nice and quiet, I thought, thinking of Rinpoche sitting somewhere on the other side of the monastery in complete silence. I peered past the open door into complete darkness and felt a surge of fear snaking through my stomach. I heard a low whimper, and saw Mo-Mo standing rigidly and looking into the darkness with wide, alert eyes.

"Ready?" Yeshi asked.

His face was tight and somber, and I could see he was scared too. I was glad he wasn't one of those guys who felt the need to pretend they weren't afraid of anything.

I set my backpack on the floor, unzipped it, and handed the first lantern to Yeshi. Then I switched on my own and stood up.

"Ready," I said.

Yeshi stepped through the doorway, and in one moment passed from the light of the kitchen window into complete blackness. Ignoring Mo-Mo's low whimper, I stepped through the doorway too.

The light from my lantern caught the back of Yeshi's head as he descended what was not so much a staircase as a series of wooden boards on a frame. Between each board was nothing but inky darkness. I felt a quick twinge of vertigo and steadied myself, making sure one foot was planted firmly before moving the other foot downward.

The air grew cool and damp, and smelled of soil and rock. I felt as if I were going into the heart of Gollum's cave in *The Hobbit*. On my right side, I brushed against wall, but there was no banister on my left, nothing to stop me from plunging over the side. I continued to negotiate the stairs with great caution, but I was still afraid I was going to fall.

"It's only fourteen stairs," Yeshi said, "then the floor. I counted yesterday. The boards are small but strong, not rickety. Don't worry."

"Okay," I said. My voiced sounded little and shaky in the dark. Pretty much matching the way I felt. I turned around and shone the light up the steps, surprised and dismayed to find that Mo-Mo had not followed us down. I stood frozen for a moment.

"I'm on the bottom now. See, Jax? It's okay, you're doing fine."

There were three more steps, then Yeshi's face was illuminated by twin pools of light from our collective lanterns, and I exhaled with relief at the feeling of solid ground under my feet. I felt the brush of Yeshi's hand on my arm — a quick, comforting squeeze. He swung his lantern up and toward the interior of the room.

"Check it out!" he said excitedly.

I raised my lantern too and caught my breath.

Chapter Five

Against both walls, several rows deep, were wooden crates. Each row was stacked four or five crates high, with smaller ones on top. There was space along the center that created a dirt aisle, allowing enough space for a person to walk the length of the room.

"What is all this stuff?" I asked.

"Gifts for Rinpoche's teacher," Yeshi said. "I opened one of them when I first came down here. Look what was inside!"

He reached for one of the small boxes closest to the stairs and lifted off its top. Then he pulled something out, holding it directly in front of me.

It was a shiny black box covered with delicately painted illustrations. The painting on top was of a triangular blue mountain capped in snow, rising out of a line of smaller green hills.

"Open it and look inside," Yeshi said.

The underside of the lid was also painted. I could make out a man in a straw hat walking on a path toward a pagoda-like building of red with a sloping black roof.

Under the painting was lettering that looked Japanese or Chinese. The interior of the box was lined with faded red velvet, and there were little compartments and drawers in which to put things.

"There's a knob on the outside — when you wind it up, the box plays music," Yeshi said, placing it gently back in the crate.

"It's beautiful," I said. "There's something like that in every single one of these?"

"I don't know," Yeshi said. "Maybe. Probably. That's why I want to look inside them."

"And you think the statue of Tsiu Marpo —"

Yeshi's hand flew up like a traffic cop signaling *stop.*

"Better not say his name in here," he said. "Just to be careful."

I swallowed. So this was one of those He Who Must Not Be Named deals. Great.

"Okay. You think the statue Rinpoche is looking for could be in one of these boxes?"

Yeshi nodded. "It would be a good place to make something hard to find."

"Like hiding a tree in the forest," I said quietly.

Yeshi gave me a surprised look. "Yes," he said. "Yes, exactly like hiding a tree in the forest! You have the wisdom of a sage, Jax."

I flushed with pleasure, glad the darkness hid the color of my face. Why did I keep turning red and getting flustered? I wasn't entirely sure what Yeshi meant by *sage*, but he clearly wasn't talking about the spice, and I knew it was some kind of compliment.

"So what do we do, just start opening them one at a time?" I asked.

Yeshi nodded. "As long as we promise we won't take anything, and we put everything back the way it was, we can do this with a clear conscience," he answered. "Because our intention is only to help Rinpoche."

"Did Rinpoche say we could do this?" I asked.

Yeshi chewed on his lower lip for a moment. "No," he said. "But he didn't say we couldn't, either. I need to help him, and if the statue is here and I can find it for him, that is what I have to do."

Then he closed his eyes, pressed his hands together and murmured softly, words I couldn't understand rapidly strung together. When he opened his eyes, he saw me staring at him.

"For protection," he said, simply. "And to offer respect."

I nodded as if that made perfect sense, because it kind of did. "You know what else we could do?" I asked. "We could take a few pictures of the way the room looks now. That way we can be absolutely sure everything is back in the right place when we're done."

"Great idea!" Yeshi exclaimed. "I don't have a camera, though."

"I do," I said. "I have one on my phone."

I pulled it from my pocket, checked to see that the flash was on, then took several photographs of the crates from various directions. When I had four or five good ones, I stood on the second step from the bottom, leaning back against the wall, and took one final picture that managed to capture pretty much the entire contents of the room.

"Okay, I think I've got enough," I said.

"Good," Yeshi said firmly. "Now we open box number two!"

After placing the crate with the black lacquered music box on the ground, Yeshi pried the lid off the second crate with a screwdriver he produced from a loop at his belt. A smell like old newspaper wafted out, and looking over Yeshi's shoulder, I could see that was exactly what the box was packed with. Yeshi stuck his hand right into the middle of it all and rummaged around.

"Got something!" he said excitedly.

It was wrapped in white cloth, like a tiny mummy. Yeshi unraveled it carefully, then exclaimed at what lay inside.

"A dagger!" I said.

"A *purbha*," Yeshi corrected, turning it over in his hand to examine it, his expression fascinated. "Ceremonial dagger. Very old, and very precious, for the lama to use in a ritual. But it isn't made to hurt any living creature.

See, the blade isn't sharp," he pointed out, poking it against his finger to show me.

The blade was discolored with age, but the handle was gold, set on four sides with a turquoise-colored stone carved into the shape of a face. Almost on impulse, I pulled out my phone again and took a picture of the *purbha* as it lay in Yeshi's hand.

"Good thinking," Yeshi said approvingly. "We can look for the statue and make a record of everything else that is here for Rinpoche to bring to Tibet. How do you keep coming up with such good ideas?"

I laughed. "I have no idea," I said. "I read a lot of mysteries. Maybe that helps."

"I love books," Yeshi said, rewrapping the *purbha* in its white cloth and putting it back in the crate. "I wish I had mysteries to read."

"Oh, I'll bring you some. I have tons!" I said.

"You will? Really?" he asked eagerly.

"I'll bring some tomorrow," I said. *Great, way to invite myself to visit,* I thought. "Oh, I mean not necessarily tomorrow, but if you invite me back, I can bring them then."

"But can't you come every day?"

I smiled. "If it's okay, I'd love to come every day. And if it's okay with Rinpoche."

Yeshi grinned. "It's okay with Rinpoche, don't worry," he said. "He likes you. Ready for the next crate?"

"Open her up," I said, wondering if Rinpoche had actually said that he liked me or if Yeshi was just guessing.

Though it was the largest crate of the three, Yeshi had a hard time finding anything in it at all. Finally, he pulled something out and stared at it, frowning with curiosity. Then he held it out.

It looked like a pair of slippers. Black-soled, the slippers were made of a gaudy red material, and crudely embroidered on the top of each one was a bright yellow bird. They were enormous — I'd never seen slippers that large. They were also, in my opinion, well . . . not very beautiful.

"Ugly! Yuck!" Yeshi exclaimed, waggling the slippers at me. "Big ugly slippers for giant feet. Maybe they came from a clown!"

I laughed, relieved that not everything we found was rare and precious. It felt good to hear the sound of laughter echoing off the walls. I was more at ease now, but the dark and chilly chamber still gave me the creeps.

We managed to open and examine a total of ten crates, when Yeshi said it was time to go back up. In addition to the first three, there was one large jade dragon, a rhinoceros horn set in silver, a disintegrating stack of parchment sheets that had probably contained ancient texts or paintings, a bolt of faded cloth, a pair of old binoculars, a bag of coins, and a pocket watch.

Stepping into the sunny kitchen was like crossing over into a different and more familiar world. Mo-Mo was sitting exactly where we'd left him and thumped his tail wildly when he caught sight of us. The air felt lovely and dry, and when Yeshi closed the door and I heard the click of the lock sliding back in place, I relaxed, only then realizing how tense I'd been.

"Should I come back at the same time tomorrow?" I asked as we walked down the hall that led to the monastery door.

"Yes, it's good," Yeshi said. "Or come earlier if you like to sit and watch the prayer flags. We will be painting mani stones too. You can see some of those tomorrow."

"What are mani stones?" I asked.

Yeshi handed me my shoes. "Find out tomorrow," he said with a small smile, brushing his hair off his forehead with his hand. I returned his smile as I took the shoes, and bent to put them on quickly. I stood up just as the door to the shrine room opened and Rinpoche himself came into the hall.

"Welcome," Rinpoche said, regarding me with merry eyes.

"Jax is going to bring me mystery novels tomorrow!" Yeshi said.

Rinpoche laughed and said something to him in Tibetan.

"I always make sure I leave enough time for my studies," Yeshi said, grinning and standing up very straight.

Rinpoche turned to me, and spoke in halting English. "You are welcome, Jax . . . every time?"

He looked to Yeshi.

"Anytime," Yeshi corrected.

"Yes. Welcome anytime," Rinpoche said.

"Thank you," I said. I felt both flustered and fascinated in his presence. "I'm glad you're here. I love the Tangyeling Monastery. And I'm sorry that your teacher never got to see it."

He smiled again, and nodded, then turned to Yeshi, making prayer hands and a little bow. "May Rinpoche see long and healthy life," he said.

Yeshi made prayer hands too. Then he opened the door, which I guess was my cue to go.

When we were outside in the sunlight, Mo-Mo trailing behind us, I asked Yeshi a question. "Why does Rinpoche call himself by his own name?"

"Ah, he means a different Rinpoche, his teacher."

"Oh," I said. "So . . . his teacher was named Rinpoche too?"

Yeshi shook his head, smiling. "No. Rinpoche's name is Tenpa Jampa. Sometimes, Tibetans use their last name like you use your first. So he is called Jampa. Rinpoche is what we call a special kind of teacher, a very important one who is passing down very old teachings. So he is Jampa Rinpoche. And his teacher is also called Rinpoche."

"Wow, I have a lot to learn," I said. "I hope you don't mind explaining things to me. Just tell me if my questions get irritating."

Yeshi stopped and fixed me with a serious look. "Tibet is the most important thing in the world to me," he said. "Every question that you ask makes my heart happy. You can ask about Tibet until the end of time, and I will never be irritated."

I struggled to find something to say, taken aback by the emotion in Yeshi's face. "Okay, I will," I said. "Um, see you tomorrow, Yeshi."

"See you tomorrow, Jax," he echoed.

I looked back once, just as I was about to turn from the monastery path onto Lotus Trail. Yeshi was lifting the lid off of the well. The outline of the monastery looked incredibly clear in the afternoon light. A ray of sunshine caught a windowpane and made it gleam like a diamond. The line of prayer flags fluttered against a sky that looked bluer than I could ever remember seeing it. *I don't want to leave,* I thought. *It's so peaceful here — everything seems to be in its right place.*

In spite of my feelings, I turned onto Lotus Trail and picked up a brisk pace. I didn't want to give my mother any more reason to worry about me. Not now, especially not now, when Yeshi had said exactly what I hoped to hear — that I could come to the monastery every single day. I couldn't risk her not letting me come back, not when I had a new friend. And not when we had a demon to find.

My dad was pulling into the driveway just as Mo-Mo and I came off of Lotus Trail.

"Look at you two," he said with a smile as he got out of the car. He walked down the driveway toward us. "Been hiking?"

"Yeah, we've been up at the monastery!"

"Monastery?" he asked. "What monastery?"

When I reached my father, I linked my arm through his.

"Dad, I hiked up the mountain with Mo-Mo this morning, and someone had cleared the path to the old building, so I went to have a look, and there's an old Tibetan monk and his student staying there! They're reopening the building. I got the whole story. It's a Tibetan monastery — Tangyeling Monastery. It was built something like thirty years ago for the monk's teacher who was coming to America, but then the teacher died. So the monastery was closed up tight all this time. But now the teacher has . . . there's a new teacher who is going to come, I think, and Yeshi and Rinpoche are fixing everything up and repainting. They're so cool, Dad! And the best thing is, Yeshi is my age, and he's teaching me about Tibet and prayer flags and everything!"

My father laughed at my enthusiasm.

"Wow, so you've had quite a day so far, kiddo! It all sounds really exciting. And I guess you solved the mystery of our mountain dog, here?"

"Actually, they'd never seen Mo-Mo before either! Were you able to talk to the vet?" I asked.

"Yes, I was," my father told me. "But he hasn't heard of any Tibetan mastiff reported missing. He says he's never even seen a pure-blooded Tibetan mastiff before. He's going to put the word out, though. Something will turn up."

I felt relief and a surge of happiness. For now, Mo-Mo would stay with me, then. But only if my mother didn't decide he had to go. And that was a big if. I needed Dad on my side for this one.

"He seems happy to hang out with me for now," I said. "Do you think that will be okay with Mom?"

My father chuckled. "Well, he'll have to keep a low profile," he said, then he paused to consider Mo-Mo's massive size. "But he certainly hasn't caused any trouble yet. He's been perfectly behaved. Yes, I think I can help smooth the way with your mom," he reassured me.

I stopped walking, since we had almost reached the house. With his arm still linked in mine, my father stopped too.

"Dad, Mom's been acting more kind of . . . you know. Anxious. I mean, I totally understand why and everything, but it's been like a year now. I feel she gets worried every time I leave the house. To be totally honest, she didn't seem happy when I told her about the monastery, and I'm afraid she's going to forbid me to go back up there. For no real reason, except for, you know."

Dad stood lost in thought for a moment. Then he led me back several yards toward the road and turned to face me.

"What happened last summer was very frightening for all of us," he said, quietly and firmly.

My eyes filled with tears, and I felt nausea gnawing at my stomach.

"But it wasn't your fault, Jax," my father added quickly. "And your mother knows that as well as I do, believe me. Mom and I were both home, and neither of us noticed when Kizzy wandered outside. And I know your mom agonizes over that. It wasn't more than four or five minutes before we realized Kiz was missing, but that's how tragedy hits sometimes.

"As many times as we tell ourselves we had no way of knowing she'd decided to go out and wade in the creek, no way to know the runoff was so heavy from the rain that she'd be swept off her feet — no matter how many times we tell ourselves that, it doesn't change what happened."

"But Kizzy is okay," I said, tears spilling over my cheeks. "You got to her in time! You pulled her out, and she's okay!"

My father enveloped me in a bear hug, pressing his hand to the back of my head.

"You're absolutely right, Jax. And that's what we need to focus on and be thankful for. In the end, we were vigilant enough to get to Kizzy in time. But your mom is still stuck in a place where she's only thinking *Kizzy almost drowned*. You and I, we've got to be patient with her, and help her get to the place where she's thinking *Kizzy is safe now*. Until she gets to that place, she's going to be stuck in all this fear and anxiety. And unfortunately, her way of dealing with it is to try to keep you and Kizzy right where she can see you all the time. She's afraid if she takes her eyes off you, something else is going to happen." He pulled back and held me by the shoulders. "I know it doesn't make sense and it's very frustrating for you. Think how hard it must be for her to be so worried all the time."

I wiped the tears from my cheeks and looked up at my father.

"You're right," I said. "I know that. And I will try to be patient, I promise. I'm just . . . It can get kind of lonely up on the mountain in the summer, and you're at work most days and it takes too long for Mom to always drive me somewhere. The monastery is just up the mountain, and I can walk there myself. I love it there, and Yeshi is my friend now. I'm just so scared Mom is going to crack down and decide there's some big danger at Tangyeling, and tell me I can't ever go see Yeshi and Rinpoche again."

My father smiled down at me, pulling a stray strand of hair out of my face.

"I'll try to back you up on that one, Jax," he said reassuringly. "I promise. As long as it's truly safe up there — as long as there's no forest fire on the mountain, or flesh-eating monster rampaging in the night, then you have my approval to visit the monastery as long as you're welcome."

"It isn't even fire season," I said quietly.

"Nope, and it won't be, if we keep getting rainstorms every week," he said, putting his arm around me and leading me back up the driveway toward the house. He didn't ask for any reassurance that there was no monster roaming the mountain at night.

After dinner was over and the dishes were cleared away, and after Kizzy was given her third bath of the day following a finger-painting malfunction, I finally retreated to my room and curled up on my bed. Mo-Mo stretched out on the floor nearby. I uploaded my pictures to my laptop and flipped through them, one by one, laughing.

I hadn't noticed Yeshi had been pulling faces as I was snapping pictures of the crates. He had photobombed every shot. In one, he had his face scrunched up and his tongue out, as if he'd tasted something horribly sour. In another, his mouth was wide open and his eyes wide, as if he were on a roller coaster. In another, he had a loopy smile and crossed eyes and one finger pointing in the air.

It was only in the last photo that I took from the steps that Yeshi wasn't doing something funny. The picture had caught him turning his head, about to look at something behind him. The combined light of the lanterns and the flash of my camera cast his shadow on the ground behind him, elongated as if the shadow were lying down in the aisle.

Looking at the picture more closely, I saw a second shadow had been cast on the far wall of the chamber. Was Yeshi holding something up to make a kind of shadow puppet?

I enlarged the picture and used some of the photo program tools to clarify and sharpen the image. There was definitely a shadow there, but Yeshi's arms were at his sides. He wasn't casting the shadow, and I couldn't see anything else in the room that could have caused it — there was nothing but the flat tops of crates.

I examined the shadow more closely. The top half was more or less shaped like a person, though the blobby circle at the top was too out of proportion to be a normal-size head. Near the bottom, though, the shape skirted out, then became four distinct lines, like the legs of a table, or an animal. *Or a horse,* I thought, and I felt the blood drain from my face at the same moment my heart began pounding so hard I thought it would break out of my chest. The more I looked at it, the more the shape became identifiable to me. It was a large figure riding on horseback.

Tsiu Marpo.

Chapter Six

For the second morning in a row, I woke up super early. Was this the new me, up before breakfast every day? I accepted that I was awake for good but decided not to get out of bed yet. It was gray and drizzling a little outside, and I was cozy under the covers. Mo-Mo was still sprawled on the floor nearby, and though he opened his eyes and watched me pull various books and my laptop onto the bed, he made no move to stand up. Good. I'd cocoon it for a while.

I tried to read the book I was in the middle of — a mystery about a girl who moves to Alaska only to find something sinister lurking in the wilderness — but I had trouble concentrating. I kept thinking about the shadow in the picture I'd taken. The one that should not, *could* not be there. Putting the book aside, I opened my laptop and pulled up the photo again. Maybe my imagination had simply gotten the better of me the night before.

But no. The more I looked at the photograph, the more I felt I was really seeing something — for lack of a better word — supernatural. *But you don't really even know what the demon looks like,* I told myself, *other than Yeshi's description.* I decided to Google Tsiu Marpo. It took me countless tries just to get the spelling close enough to get an accurate hit. When I finally got the right letter combination, I was disappointed to see that there wasn't much on the Internet about the demon, other than several scholarly articles that seemed a bit out of my realm, and a drawing of a red-faced creature riding something that looked more like a dragon than a horse. I was about to give up, then on a whim I Googled "Tsiu Marpo missing statue."

The very first hit was a link to an archived newspaper article with the headline PRICELESS TIBETAN STATUE STOLEN. I clicked through to read the article.

An ancient statue was reported stolen from the Samye Monastery in Tibet. The statue, of a little-known protector demon called Tsiu Marpo, was carved from fragments of a meteorite thought to have collided with Earth some fifteen thousand years ago. Before its theft, the statue had been made available to visiting researchers from the University of London, who determined that it was carved from remnants of the Chingha meteorite, which struck a mass of land in eastern Siberia. Researchers classified the statue's material as ataxite, the rarest form of meteorite known on the planet.

Meteorites were venerated by many ancient cultures and

accorded an array of magical powers, making sacred relics carved from ataxite especially worshipped and feared. Legends associated with this particular piece allege that the statue at various times displayed the power of speech and independent movement. The team of experts was able to date the statue to the eleventh century, predating the advent of Buddhism in Tibet. The combination of the statue's unusual subject, its age, and its ataxitic composition make the value of the piece impossible to calculate. Access to the statue was given only with the provision that it not be photographed, so the size and appearance of the statue are not known.

"This is the kind of artifact that museums and collectors wait a lifetime to acquire," said Thomas Bell, assistant to the chief curator of the Tibetan Collection at the London Museum of Antiquities. "But it's not something that should ever have left Samye. This statue was of central importance to the monastery. It is mentioned in a fourteenth-century prophecy as an object of unimaginable power. The theft was specifically predicted in the prophecy, along with a warning of the dire consequences to be suffered if the artifact did not regain its rightful place at Samye."

At this time, sources report that there are no leads regarding the identity of the thief, and the whereabouts of the statue remain unknown.

Wow. Could this actually be the statue that Yeshi and Rinpoche were looking for? I checked the date of the article — October 23, 1984. It seemed too big a coincidence that there would be two important Tsiu Marpo relics stolen from Tibetan monasteries. But Yeshi hadn't said anything about a prophecy, or unimaginable power, or dire circumstances. . . . How much did he really know about the relic we'd been searching for? And the stuff about the statue moving, and talking — was that for real? I scanned the article again, wishing there were some details about its appearance. We had absolutely no idea how big this thing was, for example. Would the Tsiu Marpo statue fit in my hand? Or would I fit in its?

I downloaded the article to my phone. I didn't know if I should show it to Yeshi or not. Yeshi himself had said Rinpoche was the one who knew the most about the statue. Surely, he'd told Yeshi whatever details he thought should be shared. But I wanted to have the article with me when I returned to Tangyeling that day, just in case. I scanned the other links that had come up in the Google search, but they were all false leads. Beyond this one article I'd found, the issue of the missing statue seemed to have been completely forgotten by everyone but Tibetans.

I was startled by the sound of someone knocking loudly on the front door of our house. I sat up in bed, listening. We lived pretty far off the beaten path. Nobody ever stopped by unannounced except the occasional lost hiker. Mo-Mo lifted his big head and froze, suddenly alert. I heard the sound of the door opening, and my father saying a muffled hello to someone. I got out of bed, walked to the window that faces the driveway, and quietly opened it several inches so I could hear better.

"What can I do for you?" I heard my father ask politely.

"My name is Gil Sandford," I heard a man's voice say. "I'm a water inspector with the Department of Environmental Protection. We're in the area taking soil samples, sir. A home owner near the base of the mountain is digging a new well, and his groundwater has tested positive for a bacterial contamination. We're trying to determine the source of it. Basic physics makes it most likely that the bacteria leeched into the soil somewhere uphill of the well."

"Bacteria?" my father asked. "What kind?"

"E. coli," the man responded. "It's not uncommon, actually. We find it a lot in areas where livestock are grazing uphill from a water source, for example. Do you raise any animals, sir? Sheep or cows, horses maybe?"

"Nope," he replied. "The only animals here are a couple of housecats and a lost dog we're taking care of until we find the owner."

"I see," the man said. "The source is probably farther up the mountain. Are there any other residences up there, or just the old monastery?"

"We're the last house on the road," Dad told him.

"All right, then, thanks very much for your time, sir. We appreciate it. I'll just collect a soil sample and be on my way."

"No problem," Dad said. "Good luck with your detective work."

"Thanks!"

I heard the door close. Through my window, I could see a tall, red-haired man in a blue jumpsuit walking down the driveway, carrying a toolbox or something in his right hand. There was a white van parked by our mailbox, with a little Earth logo and the words DEPARTMENT OF ENVIRONMENTAL PROTECTION beneath it. When the man glanced back toward the house, I dropped to the floor, my heart pounding. Mo-Mo sprang to his feet and was at my side in a split second.

"I'm okay, Mo," I said, rubbing the dog's neck. "I just got startled, that's all."

But startled by what? Some instinct had instantly warned me to avoid being seen, but why? It all seemed perfectly ordinary.

It wasn't until I heard an engine start, and the sound of the van driving away, that I could think of at least one thing that didn't seem right. The water inspector had told my father he was going to take a soil sample and go. But I had just watched him walk down the driveway without taking any samples. Had he collected it from closer to the mailbox? Or had he already collected it, then thought he ought to knock on the door and ask about the animals afterward? Either one seemed possible.

But there was something else that was nagging at me. I could feel it dancing just out of reach of my thoughts. What was it? *Stop thinking so hard,* I told myself. *Stop trying to think at all and just let your mind clear.*

I kept rubbing Mo-Mo's neck, trying to focus on nothing but the simple marvelous range of color in his abundant thick fur. There were reds and browns and golds and blacks and colors I could not even put a name to. When I was completely absorbed with nothing but the nameless shades and hues, I remembered the thing I'd been grasping for.

The DEP inspector asked about other houses up-mountain of us. His actual words were something like "any other houses, or just the old monastery." How did he know it was a *monastery*? Nobody in town had ever called it that, to my knowledge, until I had gone up there the day before.

Okay, if he was a state official, maybe he was working from state property records, and the place was listed as a monastery. That's what it was built to be anyway. Again, it was possible. The facts here might be okay. But my feelings definitely were not. Some sense or intuition was telling me that the man calling himself Gil Sandford was not who he said he was, and was not on the mountain to take soil samples. I couldn't imagine what the man really wanted, or why he would knock on our door asking about animals, but I knew there was something very wrong. I hugged Mo-Mo, wishing my father had not mentioned that we were harboring a lost dog. I didn't want that man anywhere near Mo-Mo, and I didn't want him on my mountain. But he *was* on my mountain. And he knew about the monastery.

And he might very well be heading there right now.

Chapter Seven

The drizzle of early morning became an all-out down-pour before lunch. I camped out on the living room couch with a pile of books at my side and a cat on each foot while Mo-Mo snored on the floor. For the fifth time in an hour, I checked my watch. It was eleven thirty, ten minutes later than the last time I checked. And still the rain drummed down on the roof with exasperating persistence. If it was still pouring this afternoon, I was going to have a hard time convincing my mother I had any sane reason to go hiking. But I had to get back to the monastery today — not just to keep looking for the statue but to tell Yeshi about the suspicious water inspector. What was I going to do?

Stop trying to figure it out and just let it go, I told myself. *It will work out the way it works out.*

Strange, the little sensible thoughts that have been popping into my mind recently. Yeshi and Rinpoche must be rubbing off on me.

There was a thud and a squeal, and Eliot dug his claws

into my foot as Kizzy raced into the room. Whitman gave my sister a disdainful look, then with a swish of his tail fell back asleep.

"Jax, it's boring cats and dogs outside!" Kizzy yelled.

"Pouring cats and dogs," I corrected.

"Boring," Kizzy insisted.

Yep, that was true too.

"Can't we go somewhere?" Kizzy asked. "I want to go somewhere. We never go anywhere anymore."

Also true, I thought sadly.

"Well, I'm not sure there's anywhere for us to go right now," I said. "Dad's at work, and as you noticed, it's pouring cats and dogs."

"Mom can drive us," Kizzy declared.

"She's doing something in the kitchen. We don't want to get her grumpy, right? I'll play with you, Kiz. We could play Connect Four," I suggested.

"Go. Somewhere."

Kizzy folded her arms and narrowed her eyes with determination. Then she opened her mouth and bellowed. "Mom!"

My mother appeared almost instantly in the living room door, as if she'd sprinted.

"What's wrong?" she asked, looking from me to my little sister, anxiety darkening her eyes.

"It's been boring all morning," Kizzy said, pooching

her lower lip out. "I want to go somewhere, Mom. Can we go somewhere?"

"Kizzy, stop," I said. "Sorry, Mom. I told her I'd play a game with her," I said.

"I have to GO!" Kizzy wailed.

"Why don't I drive you girls into town and treat us to lunch at Tinker's?" Mom said.

"Yeah!" Kizzy shouted, pumping one small fist in the air. "Tinker's grilled cheese and chocolate milk shake!"

"Sound okay, Jackson?" my mother asked me.

I tried not to look surprised. Mom hated doing anything on the spur of the moment. She liked everything to be scheduled in advance or she got "frazzled," as she put it. She was also usually convinced that our town was seething with criminals, all intent on kidnapping Kizzy. That also made her frazzled — I called it grumpy on a good day, and explosive on a bad one. Normally, I'd jump at the chance of a Tinker's milk shake, but I was preoccupied with getting to the monastery on time. I glanced at the clock, trying to calculate what time we'd be back even if the service was super slow.

"Jackson, are you going to answer me?" my mother asked. "I'm doing what you want, I'm making an effort, and you're just standing there like you're trying to figure out how to get out of this."

Dad must have talked to her, I thought.

"No, not at all!" I said quickly. "It's an awesome idea. Come on, Kiz, let's get your slicker and boots," I said, herding my jubilant sister toward the coat closet.

"I want to wear the orange one!" Kizzy announced. It was her new mantra — she wanted everything to be orange these days. Last year it was pink.

"Okay, but don't blame me if someone mistakes you for a fruit and tries to squeeze the juice out of you," I told her.

"I guess I should put Mo-Mo in my room?" I asked my mother, hating to do anything to remind her of his presence.

"Jackson, what's the status of this dog situation?" my mother asked me while Kizzy was absorbed in searching the bottom of the closet for one of her boots. The fact that she referred to Mo-Mo as "this dog situation" was not a good sign.

"Well, Dad called the vet to get the word out," I said. "I guess we could make posters."

She nodded.

"I'm really not comfortable having a strange animal in the house," she said.

"I know," I said, keeping my voice even. But seriously? Mo-Mo had been in our house for more than a day now, and he had been perfectly behaved. So it didn't really make sense to call him a "strange animal" any longer, right? I took a calming breath.

"But I promise you, he's totally safe. You can see how good he's been so far, right? And did you know that Tibetan mastiffs are prized guard dogs? In Tibet, they'd call him a 'defender of women and children.'"

"Mmmm," my mother murmured, giving Mo-Mo a suspicious look. "That means the breed can be aggressive to humans, then. I want to be very sure you're doing everything you can to find that animal's rightful owner as soon as possible."

"I am," I said, uncomfortable with the lie. The truth was, I personally hadn't done anything to find Mo-Mo's owner. I hadn't even remembered to ask Dad to call the vet, though he'd done it anyway. "But in the meantime, I promise you, Mo-Mo will be perfectly behaved."

"Mo-Mo?" my mother asked.

"That's his name. I mean, that's what I'm calling him anyway."

"I don't know why you need to give an animal a name when it doesn't belong to you."

I bit my lip. *I must not lose my temper,* I reminded myself. That only makes things worse, every single time. And I was so, so tired of having fights with my mother.

"I'm ready," Kizzy sang.

She looked sort of adorable in her traffic-cone orange slicker and neon-green turtle boots, which looked slightly askew.

"Are those boots on the right feet?" I asked, folding my arms and giving her a sobering look.

Kizzy dropped her head, examined her feet, and then her mouth dropped open in a little O of dismay.

"I'll change them!" she cried, plopping to the floor and wrestling the boots off her feet.

"Good job," I said. "Mo, you need to wait in my room, okay?"

Mo-Mo stood up and walked with me down the little hallway. At my doorway, he walked into the room, sat down by my bed, then slid down until his head was on his paws. His eyes fixed on mine as I lingered a moment to take in the enormous beauty of him. Then I pulled the door quietly shut.

"Sorry, I'm ready to go now!" I called as I saw Kizzy with one hand on the front doorknob, practically exploding with impatience to get moving.

"Kizzy, don't run," my mother warned. Kizzy proceeded to do the best impression of a person walking very fast but not technically running that I'd ever seen.

Fifteen minutes later, we were tucked cozily in a window booth at Tinker's. As usual, it smelled like heaven — the rich calming smell of home-cooked comfort food. I sat on one side of the table sipping a cold glass of ice water while Kizzy colored the puzzles and games on the kids' paper menu, and our mother looked around, trying to get the waitress's attention.

"Mom, can I get curly fries too? Mom, can I?" Kizzy asked.

"You won't leave any room for your milk shake," I teased.

"I will," Kizzy argued. "Fries go in my lunch aisle. Milk shakes go in my dessert aisle!"

I admired her logic.

"I don't want you to get a stomachache later," my mother said.

"I won't! Curly fries, curly fries," sang Kizzy, bouncing up and down to the beat of her own drummer.

My mother shot a look over her shoulder to see if someone was sitting in the booth behind her and my sister. I might not have noticed him otherwise.

"Cassandra, stop bouncing," my mother quietly admonished. "There's someone at the next table and you'll shake his seat."

He was facing in the other direction, so I could see only the back of his head. But there was a light directly over his table, and the dark sky outside the window reflected the inside of the restaurant like a mirror.

It was him — the man claiming to be from the DEP.

It was so bright and cheerful in the restaurant, so . . . normal, that as our food was set before us and I took the first heavenly bite of grilled cheese and tomato, I began to wonder if I hadn't simply been overwhelmed by an overactive imagination that morning. Just because something wonderful had happened to me didn't mean that something bad was going to follow. Why was I so convinced that the red-haired DEP man was an impostor who meant harm, some renegade dog thief searching for Mo-Mo? Why, for that matter, was I so afraid my mother would ban me from visiting the monastery ever again?

"This is so delicious," I said, smiling at my mother. "Does it seem like some foods taste better on rainy days? Because I could swear this is the best tomato and cheese sandwich I've ever had."

My mother smiled a little. "I think I know what you mean," she said. "Split pea soup on a rainy day always tastes better than split pea soup on a sunny day."

"Chocolate shakes taste good every single salamander day," Kizzy declared.

Mom gave Kizzy a puzzled look, then looked to me, her eyebrows raised.

"Every single *solitary* day," I translated. "But I think I like salamander better."

"Salamanders like to be in the rain," Kizzy said, launching a curly fry at her mouth but missing. "They hide when it's sunny and come out to play in the rain. Maybe we'll see some!"

"No one's going outside to play in the rain, and no one is to ever go outside without telling me or Dad," my mother said, her voice suddenly tense and her brows knitted. "And, Kizzy, you are never to go outside alone — I need to be very clear so you understand that. Never, never, never."

"But Jax goes outside alone," Kizzy whined, all happy thoughts of salamanders having left her brain.

"Only to go on hikes up the mountain," I said. "Which is perfectly safe because I'm old enough to hike the trails alone. There's never anyone on them anyway."

"You saw monkeys," Kizzy corrected.

"Monks. Actually, monk, singular — just the one. Anyway, Mom, Kizzy knows that," I said calmly. "You don't have to worry."

"Well, I *do* worry," my mother said.

I sighed, but not loud enough for anyone to hear it.

The only way to help get rid of her anxiety is to not fight it, I told myself. *Fighting it just gives it more power.*

But it wasn't always easy.

"I want to see the monkeys from the mountain," Kizzy insisted.

"I bet you'll be able to sometime," I said. "If you're very very good. But until then, what are the best rainy-day things to do?"

"Finger painting, *Star Wars* LEGO, Tintin books," my sister said.

"Brushing the cat, making cupcakes, and Pete Seeger music," I added.

"Candy Land! Pokémon! Coloring books!" Kizzy said excitedly.

"See, Mom? Kizzy's got indoor stuff on her brain."

The tension began to leave my mother's face. "That all sounds great, Jackson," she said.

"You too, Jax, you have to play too," Kizzy declared.

"I already told you I'd play with you. The only thing I have to do is take Mo-Mo for a nice long walk this afternoon. He's a really big dog, and big dogs need lots of exercise — that way they're nice and calm when you bring them home. See, having a dog is a big responsibility, Kiz. If you ever get one, you have to be prepared to take care of it, which includes going for walks, rain or shine."

"Even in the snow?" Kizzy asked.

"Even in the snow," I confirmed.

"I don't ever want to get a dog, then," Kizzy said firmly.

"And don't worry, Mom," I added quickly. "I'm just going to take Mo-Mo up the usual trail — same hike we did yesterday and the day before."

"In this weather?" my mother asked.

"She has to be repencible," Kizzy said. "Because there's a dog."

"You should wear your rain poncho," Mom told me. "Just because it's summer doesn't mean you can't catch a chill."

"I will — and it might not even be raining by then!" I said.

I finished my sandwich in one large bite, trying not to look triumphant. But secretly, I was celebrating. Not only had I made sure I could get back to the monastery on schedule, but I'd gotten the subject out of the way. Now I could relax.

Kizzy was sucking on her straw as hard as she could, though she knows as well as I do that you can't rush a Tinker's milk shake.

"Your eyes are bugging right out of your head," I said, smiling and standing up. "Relax. You'll pull a muscle! I'll be right back, Mom," I added. "I'm going to the restroom."

I walked slowly past the glass case of pies and cakes and cookies, savoring the sight of all the delightfully decorated and iced goodies. A row of dog-shaped cookies reminded me of Mo-Mo waiting patiently at home, shut up in my room. *Poor guy,* I thought. On my way back from the table, I didn't let myself linger by the desserts a second time.

I caught sight of the red-haired man just as I was passing his table. Honestly, I had forgotten that he was there at all. I felt a little silly about my earlier wave of paranoia. The man glanced up at me and met my eye, probably not long enough to notice the casual smile I gave him. I was almost past him when my eyes were drawn to a notebook on his table, which he was closing. I saw the page only for a split second before he flipped the book shut. But it was long enough for me to see a sketch, a face with a sneering mouth and a hat lined with skulls. A frightening face.

The face of Tsiu Marpo.

Chapter Eight

"Did you see the mani stones?" Yeshi asked eagerly, standing in the monastery's doorway. "I can show them to you, if you want. I don't mind the rain."

"I actually need to talk to you," I said quietly. "Is Rinpoche meditating?"

Yeshi nodded, cocking his head to one side and giving me a quizzical look. "We can go in the kitchen," he said.

I took off my shoes and rain poncho inside the door. There was a towel hanging on a hook just inside the doorway. Yeshi took it and used it to rub Mo-Mo's fur and feet dry. When he put the towel back on the hook, I followed him toward the kitchen.

"What's up?" Yeshi asked. "Are you okay?"

"I don't really know where to start," I said.

"Starting with lemonade is always good," Yeshi said. "I made it myself. Sit down, Jax. I'll get it."

He sounded so much like an adult sometimes, like a miniature version of Rinpoche. I sat at the old wooden table while Yeshi opened a small cooler in the corner and pulled out a ceramic pitcher. I looked around the kitchen as he poured two glasses of lemonade. The wall hanging and table were again covering the door that led to the basement chamber. The more I looked at it, the more it seemed the door was being deliberately hidden by the placement of the things in front of it.

"Taste," Yeshi said, placing a glass in front of me. "But you have to tell me if you don't like it. I never made lemonade before!"

I took a long sip. It was tart — I was used to having it much sweeter. But it tasted good and made my tongue tingle.

"It's perfect," I said. "Yeshi, something happened this morning. I'm not exactly sure what's going on, but something isn't right."

Yeshi raised his eyebrows in surprise. "What is it?" he asked.

I took a deep breath and told him about the man from the DEP. "Something about him felt wrong to me," I concluded. "And he seemed interested in who else lived on the mountain — he asked about Tangyeling specifically."

Yeshi nodded somberly. "The man with red hair," he said. "He came here too just before the heavy rain started. Rinpoche was outside. I was putting mani stones on the wall, and I saw them. Rinpoche would not speak English to the man. He just kept shaking his head like he didn't understand. So finally, the man went away."

"He was already here?" I asked. He must have headed straight for the monastery after leaving my house.

"Yes," Yeshi confirmed. "And your bad feeling is a very *good* feeling — that is your sage speaking to you. Rinpoche would welcome anyone who came to Tangyeling. But he would not speak to this man. Rinpoche's English is not very good, but he would have understood the man and could have spoken to him. Rinpoche must have had a bad feeling also."

I put my glass down on the table and leaned toward Yeshi. "Really? Did he say anything to you, explain what he thought gave him a bad feeling from the man?"

Yeshi shook his head. "No. He only told me that if I saw the man return, I should tell him right away, even if it meant interrupting him during meditation. What do you think the man wants?"

I took a deep breath. "You know how I said I saw the man at the restaurant today? Well, when I walked past his table, I caught a quick look at a sketch he'd been working on. Yeshi, I'm pretty sure the sketch was of Tsiu Marpo."

Yeshi's eyes widened. I had forgotten that I shouldn't say the name out loud in the monastery.

"You think this man is looking for our statue?" he asked.

I nodded.

"But . . . I don't understand," Yeshi said. "The statue is very important to Tibetans, I know. But why would anyone else be interested in it?"

I decided then and there that Yeshi had to know everything I knew. I was out of my depth now.

"That's the other thing I need to talk to you about," I said, pulling out my phone. "I woke up early this morning, and I couldn't stop thinking about Tsiu — about the statue."

Yeshi looked worried. "Jax, did you see it in your dreams?"

"No," I said. "Why? If I had, would that be bad?"

"You said you were thinking about the statue when you woke up."

"I was," I said, nodding. "Because of the pictures I took yesterday. Just . . . here. Look at them yourself. Push this arrow on the screen to go from picture to picture."

Yeshi took my phone and looked at the screen. His face broke into a wide grin. He laughed out loud when he saw the second and third pictures. Then he froze, and his smile vanished, the color draining from his face.

"Buddha's breath," he whispered.

"I know what I think is in that picture," I said. "What do *you* see?"

Yeshi handed me back the phone. "His shadow," he said very quietly. "On the wall."

I nodded. "Me too."

"I remember the moment," Yeshi said. "I was making faces. Funny, ha-ha. Then I heard a sound, like something heavy falling in the distance. I turned and looked over my shoulder. But I never saw this shadow that's in the photograph, Jax!"

"What does it mean?" I asked.

"I don't know. Maybe we summoned him without realizing."

"How?" I asked.

"I do not know. A sound, the flash from your camera maybe. I know very little about him. We might have disturbed him. Or maybe he was already there, waiting."

The skin on my arms prickled at the thought.

"After I saw the picture of the shadow, I had all these questions, so I searched on the Internet to see what I could find. I found one thing, not just about the demon — it's a newspaper article about a statue of a demon. A really important one. That was stolen from Tibet."

"What?" Yeshi exclaimed. "But I have to see it. Do you remember what the article said? Could you maybe go home and get it?"

"I don't need to. I knew you'd want to see it, so I downloaded a copy of it onto my phone. Hang on, let me pull it up."

Yeshi fidgeted impatiently in his seat as I searched for the article in my downloads file.

"Here it is," I said, handing it to him. "Just run your finger over the screen when you get to the bottom and it will go to the next page."

Yeshi began to read, frowning with concentration.

"Samye," he murmured.

"What?"

"Samye Monastery," he said, glancing up at me. "Where it says the statue was stolen from. That is Rinpoche's monastery. This stolen statue in the article you found, it's the same one. It has to be. This is what Rinpoche has been looking for."

He resumed reading, an expression of amazement on his face.

I wanted to pepper him with questions, but I managed to restrain myself.

"It says, 'This is the kind of artifact that museums and collectors wait a lifetime to acquire,'" Yeshi read. He looked up at me. "I have heard about this. People come to Tibet sometimes with old guidebooks of sacred sites. Many have been destroyed — these people come to look for the ruins, hoping they will find things, statues or *tsa-tsas* or *thangkas*, the paintings on fabric like we have hanging over the door to the underground chamber. And they take them, to keep or to sell. It is very bad. Such things should stay where they are."

"Why have many sacred sites been destroyed?" I asked.

Yeshi looked away then, somewhere off in the distance.

"After the invasion. Chinese soldiers were ordered by Mao Tse-tung to destroy our monasteries."

He pressed his lips into a thin line. I could tell he didn't want to say anything else about it.

"This museum, this Thomas Bell," I said. "I wonder if we could get in touch with him. I mean, I know this article was written a long time ago. But maybe he's still there, or maybe there's somebody there who could tell us more. Like about this prophecy they mention."

"How would we do that?" Yeshi asked.

"Well, everybody has an email address. Once I was reading this really good book, and I went to the author's website, and her email address was there, so I sent her a message, and she wrote back to me the next day! So my feeling is, why not at least try?"

Yeshi nodded. "I think this is a good idea, Jax."

"I'll do it when I get home this afternoon," I said.

"I think maybe it is also a good idea for us to wait

to open any more crates, until we see if there is anything else important we must know about the statue," Yeshi said.

I felt disappointed and relieved at the same time. Yeshi noticed my expression.

"I just think we have to be extra careful," he added.

"No, I know. You're right," I assured him. "Anyway, I —"

My words were interrupted as Mo-Mo stood up suddenly, his nose in the air. He turned and trotted quickly from the room with great purpose. Yeshi and I exchanged a curious look, then followed him.

He went straight to the front door and waited as Yeshi and I slipped our shoes on. As soon as Yeshi opened the door, Mo-Mo shot through it. Following him, I saw that the rain had stopped, and the sun was shining through a break in the clouds.

Mo-Mo went down the stairs and turned left, quickly disappearing around the corner of the monastery. He seemed to be heading for the back of the building. I stopped on the bottom step. What if the red-haired man had returned and was snooping around back there? But the little wave of fear went away when I imagined anyone lurking back there looking up and seeing a massive dog galloping toward them. We were safe with Mo-Mo. I had absolutely no doubt of that. Yeshi was already almost to the corner, and I jogged a little to catch up with him, just in time to see Mo-Mo's tail disappear around the far corner.

"Do you think there's an animal back there or something?" I asked.

Yeshi didn't answer — he didn't have to, because the moment we stepped beyond the wall of the monastery, we both came to a full stop. Mo-Mo was sitting in the grass, staring over the mountain at a gorgeous rainbow shimmering in the sky.

"Oh!" Yeshi exclaimed. "It's a *ja*! Rainbow!"

"It's beautiful," I said.

"And a very good sign," Yeshi said. He gave me a funny look, then returned his gaze to the rainbow.

"What does it mean?" I asked.

"In Tibet, it could mean a great master is being reborn or is nearby, maybe a blessing from a sky deity. A good omen."

Mo-Mo hadn't moved. He sat facing the rainbow, alert but content.

"Is this why Mo-Mo rushed out of the monastery like that?" I asked. "Because of the rainbow? There isn't a window in the kitchen facing this way. How could he have possibly known?"

Yeshi gave me another long, impossible-to-read look.

"Why do you keep looking at me like that?"

"Maybe you knew, and Mo-Mo picked up on that," he said.

"But I didn't know there was a huge rainbow out here. How could I?" I asked.

"Sometimes we don't know what we know," Yeshi said.

I *really* didn't know what *that* meant, but it seemed stupid to say so.

"Don't you ever wonder why Mo-Mo is here?" Yeshi pressed.

I nodded. "Of course I do."

"Everything that happens in our lives is a signpost, if we know how to read it. Mo-Mo is here because he is supposed to be here. He is here because of you."

As if he were listening and understanding, Mo-Mo stood up and walked over to me. He sat down at my feet.

What Yeshi was saying seemed so silly I almost laughed out loud. Not the idea that Mo-Mo's appearance was out of the ordinary — that I believed completely, as I believed there was something magical up there, something in Rinpoche and in Yeshi and in the monastery itself. But the idea that this had anything to do with me — that was the silly part. I was, sadly, terminally ordinary, and Yeshi would eventually figure it out for himself. But I saw no point in going out of my way to help him realize it too soon.

"Can I see the mani stones now?" I asked.

Yeshi's face lit up like a sunburst. "Sure! We've been putting them near the prayer flags — come see!"

We left the rainbow behind, walking through wet

grass that was glimmering as the sunlight illuminated the raindrops still clinging to each blade. Mo-Mo raced ahead, galloping joyfully over the grass.

Beneath a tree where one end of the prayer flags was tied, I saw a small mound of smooth stones painted with little designs that seemed to correspond to the colors of the prayer flags.

I didn't know if I was supposed to touch them, so I bent down to have a closer look. Yeshi kneeled in the grass, picked up one of the stones, and handed it to me.

"This is Tibetan writing. It says *om mani padme hum*. This is the mantra of compassion, the most important mantra for Tibetan Buddhists. Rinpoche says all the teachings of Buddha are contained in this one mantra."

"They're beautiful," I said, turning the stone over in my hand. On the back was painted a pair of eyes.

"The wind and the rain and sun make the stones sing, so the mantra is released again and again."

I closed my hand over the stone for a moment, then opened it again.

"I love them, Yeshi," I said, holding the stone out to him.

He shook his head and grinned.

"You keep that one. Rinpoche and I will make more. By the end of the summer, you will see them everywhere!"

I opened my mouth to say no, of course I couldn't keep it, but something stopped me. I slipped the mani stone into my pocket.

"Thank you," I said.

I sat in the grass next to Yeshi even though it was still damp. We didn't speak for a while; we just sat there. The clouds were slowly disappearing and the heat of the sun increased. I felt my vision and my hearing had become incredibly sharp all at once. I was aware of every little thing around me, the movement of an ant up a blade of grass, the play of the tree's shadow across my legs, the sound of the wind through the trees picking up, then dropping away. The distant screech of a red-tailed hawk. I don't know how long we were sitting there — it might have been five minutes or it might have been twenty — when Mo-Mo stood up and I turned to see what he was looking at.

Rinpoche was walking across the grass toward us, barefoot, his deep maroon robe brushing the tips of the grass. Yeshi stood up, so I did too. Rinpoche leaned down and reached for the small mound of mani stones with his left hand. His slender wrist was wrapped in a strand of small brown beads, which glinted in the sunlight as he placed another stone in the pile.

Seeing Rinpoche this close-up, so clear in the sunlight, I realized just how old he looked. I don't mean frail or sickly — actually, he was the opposite. But I could see the age in the deep lines of his face and his paper-thin skin and elegant, tapered fingers.

"Yeshi-la," Rinpoche said, and followed with something in Tibetan, to which Yeshi responded in the same language.

They both seemed to be looking at me for a moment. Flustered, I turned away, leaning down to scratch Mo-Mo's head, a large and welcome diversion.

"It is time for me to work on my studies," Yeshi told me. "Rinpoche says you are welcome to stay here."

Rinpoche's eyes were still on me, and I met his gaze for a moment. It was hard to look away from those intelligent, smiling eyes.

"Thank you," I said. "One of these days, I'm going to do that. I could spend all day here — it feels like time is stopped on this side of the mountain."

Rinpoche raised his eyebrows and said something I could not understand, his eyes never leaving mine.

"Rinpoche says you are right, we have no time here, and we will always have no time except for this moment now," Yeshi translated.

Rinpoche kept looking at me. I felt no matter what I said, it was going to sound incredibly stupid. But it seemed rude not to answer him.

"I'm going to go home and think about that very hard," I said truthfully.

Rinpoche gave a great, booming laugh.

"It's good," he said, rubbing one hand on his head. "It is good you are, Jax-la."

I carried the sound of that deep belly laugh all the way down the mountain with me, hearing it with every step I took on the path. It was as real and solid in my mind as the mani stone in my pocket.

Chapter Nine

I usually don't leave my cell phone on when I go to bed at night, but for some reason on this night, I did. So when the email notification rang sometime after midnight, I sat up in bed, confused and curious. I picked up my phone and drew a deep, surprised breath.

I hadn't really expected anyone from the London Museum of Antiquities to answer the brief, odd email I'd sent hours earlier. Yet my inbox icon was lit with a message from LM Antiquities. Suddenly wide awake, I switched on the light and opened the letter.

Dear Jackson,

Thank you for your email regarding the stolen statue of Tsiu Marpo. I appreciate your inquiry, and enjoyed your "greetings from scenic Nolan, New York," and return to you greetings from rustic Mansfield, Connecticut, where I am a visiting speaker this month at the university, far from my London home. I have access to my museum email, and as I am the individual from the 1984 newspaper article which you referenced, I am taking the liberty of answering your inquiry personally. To answer your questions in the order they were asked:

1. The dimensions of the statue remain unknown, though for various reasons, I would estimate it to be approximately ten inches high. Given its iron ataxite composition, that would put its weight at roughly twenty-two pounds.

2. The prophecy referenced in my article is that of an eighteenth-century tulku called Khenpo Zur. I'm attaching the portion of that text that may be of interest to you with this email.

3. To my knowledge, no significant leads or information have ever come to light with regard to the fate of the statue following its theft in 1984.

4. No, I do not think this question sounds "crazy." However, it has given me pause. You want to know if the statue is dangerous. As a museum curator, I would tell you that no statue is dangerous (unless it falls on you). However, the relic we are discussing is, as you perhaps have guessed, much more than a simple statue. It is a representation of a powerful entity and, as such, must be treated with great care and respect. But it is my belief that the piece is also a terma, meant for the eyes of what we would in English call a treasure revealer. While I expect neither of us is interested in delving into an extensive summary of Tibetan history, I will summarize. The Great Teacher Padmasambhava brought Buddhism to Tibet in the sixth century. During his lifetime, he hid away a number of powerful treasures and teachings throughout Tibet. Collectively, we call them termas, though they can take many forms, from actual scrolls buried in mountain

caves to hidden messages on, or sometimes inside, a relic such as a statue. So while the statue itself is of enormous monetary value, it is this terma that is, to the monks of Samye, a treasure of incalculable value. For many reasons, it would be unthinkable for this terma to fall into the wrong hands. Unfortunately, for this very reason, relics such as this are highly prized, which leads me to your final question.

5. Yes, I believe there are individuals in many countries (most certainly including America) who would do anything to get their hands on the atax-ite Tsiu Marpo. Though the acquisition and resale of such an artifact would be strictly illegal, this kind of thing happens all the time in the thriving international black market for rare antiquities. I understand, as you have emphasized, that all of your questions are hypothetical. So I too will close with a hypothetical warning. Should an individual have reason to believe they know the location of such a relic, and should this individual have reason to believe that a suspicious person may be trying to illegally acquire such a relic, the greatest possible caution should be taken. There are those who would stop at nothing in such a hunt.

I appreciate your inquiry. If you have any further questions or concerns, be they hypothetical, fantastical, or mundane, please do not hesitate to contact me again via email, or by mobile telephone at the number listed below.

With very best regards,
Dr. Thomas Bell

Wow. I had the increasingly familiar feeling that I was in a movie or a novel. But this was very real. I had sent my short email to the General Information and Questions link on the museum website I found. I never imagined Thomas Bell would now be the curator thirty years later, or that he would answer my email himself, and in such great detail. It was obvious to me that Dr. Bell had taken my "hypothetical" questions very seriously. Had I been wrong to contact him?

But Yeshi was the one who said it was a good idea, I reminded myself. And Dr. Bell had just provided a lot of very helpful information. And what about the prophecy? He said he had sent it. I found the attachment icon on the email and clicked on it. The attachment contained an excerpt of only a few paragraphs, with a section highlighted.

Six snakes coil at the root of the black tree when ocean walkers plunder the snow caves and gompas *on the rooftop of the world. With the last breath of the mountain abbot is lost the hidden word of the Lotus-born. When the moon-marked boy rides the sky ship into the setting sun, a sleeping demon will stir. Then comes a protector to the innocent with eyes of lapis, and he shall be guardian and protector to this* dakini, *and together they are as an army. Beneath a skyless void lies the treasure, and the hidden memory awaits in a door that clatters below twenty-eight feet. Shall the Rightful Teacher open the door, the demon Dharma*

*protector shall slumber, but the hand of the Ocean Walker will
ignite his wrath, and all the afflictions of the dark age will prosper, and the blood of the Precious One shall be spilled.*

I read it again, puzzled. This was the prophecy Dr.
Bell had referred to? Not one word of it made any sense
to me. I made sure my phone saved the document so I'd
be able to show it to Yeshi later. Then I read Dr. Bell's
email again. Something about his tone and the way he
put together his sentences made me feel I would like him
very much if I ever met him. My eyes fell on his warning: *The greatest possible caution should be taken.* His meaning
was crystal clear to me: The red-haired man could be
very dangerous.

I have to make sure Yeshi and Rinpoche understand that, I
thought, my eyelids suddenly heavy. *I have to make sure
they're on guard. Warn them. Greatest possible caution . . .*

Somewhere in the middle of repeating that thought to
myself, I fell asleep. I didn't feel I was asleep, but I must
have been, because all at once, I was sitting at the mouth
of a cave high up on a mountain. The air was crisp, the
sky magnificently spacious, and the sound of rushing
wind surrounded me. Far below lay a lush green valley,
and in its center was a lake of shimmering turquoise. I
looked down and saw that I was wearing red robes, and
had a string of dark brown beads around my left wrist. I
smelled smoke and the scent of sweet incense, and turned

around to see a fire in a small stone circle burning in the cave. On the wall of the cave were painted the colored symbols I'd seen on Yeshi's mani stones. I could make out a figure through the smoke, moving through the cave toward me, a lean figure in crimson robes with a young, joyful face and eyes as dark as night. *Rinpoche,* I heard myself say to him in the dream. And that is all I remember, except that I also felt great happiness, as if I were at home, where I was meant to be, not the cave itself but at the side of the young man. At home in a mountain cave with this stranger I called *Teacher.* Rinpoche.

I awoke to the sound of singing outside, near my window. Kizzy? I looked at the clock — it was barely past seven in the morning. What was she doing up, and why was she outside? I got out of bed and walked over to my window. Kizzy was sitting on the paved path that led to the driveway, surrounded by stubs of colored chalk. She was drawing a picture and singing to herself happily. The sky was dark, and I heard a distant rumble of thunder.

Harmless, but Mom would freak out if she caught Kizzy outside the house unattended. I knew I'd better go out there, though I hated to get out of bed after my odd, interrupted night's sleep.

I pulled on my jeans, and Mo-Mo stood up expectantly.

"Yep, we're gonna go check on her," I said. "I just need a sweatshirt — it feels cold this morning!"

I rummaged around in my closet and pulled out a large faded Kenyon College sweatshirt that my dad had given me. Slipping my feet into my sandals, I was reaching for my cell phone when I heard something that stopped me in my tracks. Mo-Mo was growling — a deep, threatening sound that made my heart skip a beat. This dog had been almost perpetually by my side for two days, and I'd never heard him make a sound like that. I ran back to the window and looked outside. Kizzy was gone.

"Come on!" I called to Mo-Mo, opening my bedroom door and moving as quickly and quietly as I could to the front hall. When I opened that door, Mo-Mo shot through it and bounded around the side of the house. I ran after him.

The first thing I saw when I reached the yard was Kizzy, and I almost yelled with relief. But then I saw that she wasn't alone. A man stood facing her, his back to me. A man in a blue jumpsuit — a man with red hair. Mo-Mo galloped toward them, leaping to Kizzy's feet and spinning to face the man. Mo-Mo bared his teeth and snarled, and the man stumbled backward.

"Get away from my sister!" I yelled across the yard.

The man turned around and looked relieved when he saw me.

"Hey, can you please call your dog?"

I narrowed my eyes and walked closer to Mo-Mo.

"I think he's fine right where he is," I said. Mo-Mo snarled again.

"Okay, look — I think there's a misunderstanding here. I work for the Department of Environmental Protection. I'm collecting soil samples — your father knows me," the man said, glancing nervously between me and Mo-Mo.

"You were supposedly here *yesterday* for your soil sample," I said, my voice tight. I didn't want to scare Kizzy, but I wanted this man to know I wasn't buying his story.

"He's looking for treasure!" Kizzy exclaimed excitedly. "He invited me to go on a treasure hunt with him on the mountain! Where the monkeys are!"

The blood drained from my face. Invited Kizzy to go with him?

The man laughed nervously.

"Wow, kids can really jumble things! I was just explaining to your sister that I'm looking for a bacteria, which is kind of like going on a treasure hunt."

I walked straight over to the man as if I were a man myself, not a skinny twelve-year-old girl. I jabbed my finger at his face.

"I know what you're looking for," I hissed. "I know exactly what you're doing here, and I know you don't work for the DEP. You better leave this mountain and not come back, or I'll call the cops."

The vaguely confused and innocent expression disappeared from the man's face, replaced by a dark, threatening look.

"You need to mind your own business," he said. "No cop is going to buy some crazy story from you."

"You need to stay off my mountain," I said. "What's up there doesn't belong to you. You're a thief and a liar and you're looking for something to steal so you can sell it for lots of money. I'm way ahead of you. I know what you're looking for. It's somewhere you'll never find it."

The man's eyes narrowed.

"No one knows where it is yet," he said, "but I know it's somewhere in that monastery."

"I know where it is," I lied. "Which is how I know you're never going to find it."

"You're lying. I will find it," he said.

"Jax, can we go on the treasure hunt? Can we?" Kizzy sang.

"Would you like to see how well I *can* lie?" I said to the man, ignoring Kizzy. "If you don't get in your car and drive *down* this mountain and away from my house right now, I'm going to scream my lungs out and tell everyone who will listen that you were trying to lure my little sister into your car. That's a story the cops will take very seriously. Want to see if I'm right? I'm counting to ten, and then we'll find out. One. Two."

"You're way out of your league, kid. You're messing with some very dangerous people."

"Three. Four."

He shook his head.

"This isn't over," he hissed. "I'll be back, and crying wolf won't help you then, and neither will your guard dog."

"Five. Six."

Finally, he turned and walked quickly toward the driveway.

"Seven!" Kizzy said. "Is this part of the treasure hunt?"

"Shhh," I said, walking over to Kizzy and putting my arm around her. I hoped she wouldn't notice that I was shaking. "We need to make sure he's gone."

I heard a car door slam, and an engine start.

"Stay here," I said, walking toward the driveway. I reached it in time to see the man's car driving down the mountain. Away from Tangyeling, and from Yeshi and Rinpoche.

For now.

But how much time had I bought? My shouts and threats to call the police weren't going to keep him away forever.

"He left," Kizzy said sadly. "I thought we were going to do something fun!"

I walked over to my little sister and took both her hands in mine.

"Kiz, what exactly did the man say to you?"

"I was drawing pictures. He drove by and saw me. He said he was looking for a secret treasure, and I asked him if he meant the one the monkeys on the mountain had."

"What makes you think the monk on the mountain has a treasure?" I asked.

Kizzy shrugged. "Dunno. But the man thought so too. He asked me if I'd seen it, if I could go with him and show him."

I looked away. Kizzy was five years old. And this man had no problem attempting to use her to find the statue. Dr. Bell's words came into my mind: *There are those who would stop at nothing in such a hunt.* Abducting a five-year-old was probably the least of it.

"Listen, Kiz, do you remember Stranger Danger?"

Kizzy's face grew serious and she nodded.

"Okay, you have to do the Stranger Danger rules if you see that man again."

"Is he a bad man?" Kizzy asked.

I hesitated. I didn't want to scare her. And I didn't want her repeating things to my mother. I wasn't sure what to do yet, and the last thing I needed was my mother thinking·there was a bad guy lurking around the mountain. We'd both be shut in our rooms for the rest of the summer.

"I don't know him, Kizzy. But we're going to practice, and pretend like he is. Just you and me, though. It's our secret practicing game. Okay? It's really important that you do that."

Kizzy nodded.

"Okay."

"Good. Now how about we go inside and have breakfast. I'll make you eggs and toast," I said, gently leading her toward the front door. Mo-Mo walked on Kizzy's other side, like a bodyguard.

"I want Cap'n Crunch," Kizzy declared.

"Then I will make you a huge, ginormous bowl of Cap'n Crunch," I told her.

Kizzy squealed with happiness, and I couldn't help smiling. It must be nice to get so wildly happy about little things like a bowl of sugar-soaked cereal.

Kizzy had gotten through almost half of the little mountain of cereal I'd served her, when my mother came in.

"I wish your father wouldn't buy that cereal," she said. "Isn't there something healthier Kizzy can have for breakfast?"

Kizzy's eyes grew wide. She couldn't speak because her mouth was filled with cereal, but she hugged the bowl protectively, chewing and staring at my mother with imploring, Disney eyes.

My mother laughed, and so did I. Kizzy ought to be an actress someday, with the faces she was capable of making.

"Okay, I get the point," she said. "Relax. You can keep your bowl of Captain SugarBombs, or whatever they're called. Listen, the weather report says we're supposed to get a big storm later in the afternoon. High winds, lightning, hail, the whole works. So I'm going to go into town early to get all the food shopping done, and I can stop at the post office and the dry cleaner while I'm at it. I'll get plenty of extra batteries too, in case we lose power. I'll be back in about an hour and a half, okay, Jax?"

"Sure, Mom, no problem," I assured her. But secretly, I was disturbed by the news of the storm. I had to get up to the monastery today to warn Yeshi. How could they live alone up there with no electricity and no phone? What if something happened to Rinpoche? I promised myself that when all the excitement had passed, I would persuade Yeshi to at least get a cell phone for emergencies.

"Keep an eye on your sister," my mother told me.

I nodded patiently. Like, obviously I was going to keep an eye on my sister. I hated that she had to say it every time.

"And I don't want either of you to leave the house while I'm gone either. If you need to take that animal out, stay in the yard. The mountain always gets hit first and hardest when there's bad weather."

"We'll be fine, Mom," I promised her.

"I have my cell phone with me, so —"

"Mom," I interrupted, walking over and placing a hand on her arm. "You don't need to worry. I'll watch Kizzy, and everything will be fine."

My mother's tense expression suddenly disappeared.

"Oh, of course you will, Jax. I'm sorry. I get a little nutty sometimes. You're terrific with Kizzy, and I appreciate it."

I gave her a hug. It was so nice to hear her say that, and so long since she'd said anything like it.

"Okay, I'm going to go now," my mother said. "Have fun."

"Bye, Mommy. We will be good and look for monkeys and do Stranger Danger!" Kizzy said.

"Kiz, finish your cereal before it gets soggy," I said. The more Cap'n Crunch was in her mouth, the less likely she'd be to add something I didn't want my mother to hear.

As soon as the car pulled out of the driveway, Kizzy ran crazily from room to room. Running in the house was against my mother's rules, but not mine. So I let Kizzy do it while I put away the dishes and wiped down the table, hoping she might exhaust a fraction of her wild energy. Mo-Mo lay near the kitchen door. Occasionally, Kizzy would whiz by, and his ears would prick, and he'd give me a look.

"I know," I told him. "They're like puppies at that age, right? Totally out of control."

I had just dried and put away Kizzy's cereal bowl when I heard my sister scream my name.

Chapter Ten

I raced into the front hall with Mo-Mo at my heels. I almost yelled with relief when I found Kizzy alone and perfectly fine, her hands and face pressed against the window by the front door.

"Kizzy, you almost gave me a heart attack!" I exclaimed. "Why did you scream like that?"

Kizzy whirled around. Her face was shining.

"Jax, come see. Come *see*!"

I stepped next to her and looked where one small finger was pointing, out the window and up at the sky.

It was a spectacular double rainbow. The clouds had parted overhead and a perfectly brilliant arc spanned the sky down to the mountain. Higher in the sky was a second, fainter rainbow, its flawless twin. I'd never seen a rainbow so vivid or so bright, and I'd definitely never seen a double rainbow. It almost looked too real to be real, like someone had painted it there.

Kizzy yanked open the door and stepped outside to get a better look. Mo-Mo and I followed her.

I caught my breath at the same moment Mo-Mo lifted his nose to the sky and barked three times.

One of the twin rainbows seemed to end partway up the mountain, not too far from the spot where our property ended and the woods began. The fainter rainbow's end was clearly visible. It stretched in an unbroken arch from the sky to the roof of Tangyeling.

A *ja*, I heard Yeshi say in my mind, pleased that I remembered the Tibetan word for rainbow. A good omen, Yeshi had said, a sign. But what did it mean? Maybe it was an omen that the monastery was safe. Or maybe it was a sign that they needed me — maybe Tangyeling was trying to get my attention!

Mo-Mo whined and nudged me with his nose, then trotted away across the yard toward a small figure marching toward the woods. Kizzy! I hadn't even noticed she'd left my side, I had been so busy looking at the sky.

"Kiz, come back!" I called. Kizzy stopped and turned toward me. Mo-Mo was already at her side.

"I just wanna see the rainbow's end!" Kizzy said. "We can find a pot of gold or see lettercons!"

I strode across the grass toward my sister, opening my mouth to say the word *no* and take her back inside. Mo-Mo had raised his head and was looking up at the rainbow. I didn't know dogs could see rainbows. And yet this dog seemed to be not only able to see them but to smell them too. What did a rainbow smell like?

"It's right there, Jax, see? The end of the rainbow is right there!"

Kizzy tugged my arm, her voice pleading, as she pointed toward the woods at the end of our yard. It really did look like the brightest of the rainbows was coming down right there, somewhere in the middle of the trees. It was eerie and beautiful. Everything seemed dreamlike. With dark rain clouds still covering most of the sky, it looked like the clouds had parted just so the sun could shine down on the mountain. On Tangyeling. On a day like this, maybe we really would see leprechauns.

"Jax, pleeeeeeeeeeeeeeeez?"

Oh, what would it hurt to just go and see? Just a five-minute walk into the woods and back, and only while the sun was shining.

"Okay," I said, "but no running ahead. You have to hold my hand. And only if you promise to turn around when I say we have to, even if you don't want to."

"I promise," Kizzy said, grabbing my hand and yanking me forward.

We left the yard and crossed into the line of cedar trees and evergreens. But as soon as we reached the first clearing, it looked like the rainbow was actually coming down just in the distance, in the rocky line where the creek passed through on its way down the mountain. But that too proved to be an illusion, because when we reached the rocks, the rainbow had jumped forward again.

"We have to follow it!" Kizzy shouted exuberantly.

But I had suddenly snapped out of the dream, reminded of reality by the sound of the creek burbling. This was where Kizzy had gone that day last summer. This was where she had decided to go wading, and where water had swept her off her feet. The creek looked quiet and utterly harmless at the moment, but I knew that looks could be deceptive, and that the gentle stream could turn very quickly to rushing water, especially when there was heavy rain anywhere up-mountain.

I had been irritated at my mother for not trusting me, and yet what had I done as soon as she'd left? Brought Kizzy back to the creek when heavy rain was on its way.

"Come on, we have to go back right now," I said firmly.

"But it's right there," Kizzy said, pointing. "The rainbow end is right over there!"

Do you remember what you promised? Kizzy?" I asked.

I heard her name again, in a voice that sounded like mine, coming like an echo from behind me.

Mo-Mo's ear pricked up, but he did not tense the way he had earlier when he had sensed danger. I looked around, momentarily confused.

"Kizzy? Jax?" I heard, louder this time.

Oh, no.

That was all I had time to think before my mother burst through the trees.

"Where is she?" my mother cried. "Where is Kizzy?"

Kizzy stepped around me, and into view.

"I'm right here, Mommy," she said. "Are you chasing the rainbow too?"

Mom didn't answer. Instead, she covered her face in her hands and began to cry.

No one spoke on the short walk back to the house. My mother had Kizzy tightly by the hand and was pulling her along in front of me. Kizzy glanced back once, giving me a confused look, her lower lip quivering. I wanted to kick myself. She was too little to make the connection to the rainbow and the day that must seem like forever ago when she decided to go wading and almost drowned. This wasn't her fault.

"Cassandra, go into your room and close the door," my mother said as soon as we were in the house.

"We only wanted to see the lettercons," Kizzy whispered, hanging her head as she turned and walked down the hallway to her room.

My mother gave me a terrible look.

"I can explain," I said quietly.

"You scared me to death!" she exclaimed.

"I'm sorry, I just —"

"No, you're not hearing me, Jackson. I got halfway down the mountain, realized I'd forgotten my wallet, and drove back to the house. And you were gone. Both of you. Without a trace. And I knew, I *knew* without a doubt that something terrible had happened. How did I know that? Because ten minutes before, just *ten* minutes, you looked me in the eye and promised you would take care of your sister, and you would not leave the house, and that I could trust you. But you were gone. I was terrified! Because there was no explanation for your not being in that house, other than that something had happened."

I stared at the ground.

"I said I was sorry."

"That's not good enough! How could you do that? How could you even begin to think you could take your sister into the woods after what I said to you?"

I pressed my hand over my mouth for a moment, because sometimes that helped me to not cry when I thought I might cry. Then I took a quick, shallow breath.

"We . . . the sun came out and there was this huge double rainbow. Really huge and clear, and one of them came down just on the other side of the yard. And Kizzy wanted to see it. She thought there would be a pot of gold. And leprechauns."

My mother looked even angrier. Her face had gone white, and her lips were pressed tightly together.

"I don't care if a herd of unicorns was standing smack in the middle of the driveway. I forbade you to set foot out of the house, and you deliberately defied me."

"I did not deliberately defy you," I said angrily.

"You know our rules, and you broke them," she replied, her voice going dangerously quiet.

"Your rules, new rules you came up with by the dozen after Kizzy ran off last summer," I retorted. "That had nothing to do with me, but you made your rules apply to me too. Until last summer, I was allowed to go out on the mountain on my own, as long as I told you where I was going and brought my phone. Did I ever get into any trouble? Did I ever even once leave you worrying where I was?"

"That is not the point," my mother said.

"It is the point," I cried, stomping my foot in anger. "You made it like a prison around here! And okay, I know you were really scared about what happened to Kizzy last year, I know that, okay? So I went along with it, I figured you just needed some time to get over it. But you've just been getting worse and worse! You don't want me to do anything anymore. I'm not the five-year-old, but you treat me like one!"

"And now you're acting like one!" my mother snapped. "And the minute I trust you with any responsibility, what do you do? You sneak off to the creek, and you take Kizzy with you."

"I'm sorry we scared you," I said. "But there was no danger. I made Kizzy hold my hand; I was with her every second. It's not the same thing — you're totally overreacting."

I felt something heavy and warm press against my leg. I reached down and touched the top of Mo-Mo's head, thanking him for his silent support.

"You are in no position to tell me I am overreacting," my mother told me. "I haven't even begun to react. There are going to be serious consequences for this, Jackson. I'll discuss it with your father when he gets home from work. But I can tell you right now, you are grounded. You will not be leaving this house for any reason. You will not take that animal for any walks, you will not go hiking, and you certainly won't go visiting those strange people messing around in that old building."

"It's a Buddhist monastery!" I exclaimed. "And they're monks!"

"You don't know anything about them," my mother said, shaking her head. "Anybody can throw on a robe and call themselves a monk — this could be a fringe group, a cult —"

"Are you serious?" I exclaimed. I threw my hands in the air, and turned and began walking toward my room. Then I stopped and turned back.

"You are completely blinded by paranoia — do you realize that? You sound crazy! Now this monastery you've never even seen, and these people you've never met are part of some cult? Look them up on the Internet — look up Tangyeling Monastery, look up Samye Monastery in Tibet."

"I don't care who they are. You will not go back there again."

I felt a hot surge of anger hit me dead-on. I could barely catch my breath. This was the absolute last thing I wanted to happen. This could not be.

"Mom, just talk to Dad about it, okay? He'll tell you that the monastery is fine. He'll tell you that —"

"I do NOT need your father's permission to make a decision, Jackson. You will not go back to that place. Period. End of sentence."

"You don't know what you're doing," I said. "If you'd just trust me enough to —"

"I don't trust you!" my mother interrupted. "Not now, not after what you did today. It's going to be a long time before you can earn that trust back."

"But —"

"Enough!" my mother said. "This is not a negotiation. I want you to go to your room and stay there. I do not want to see you or hear from you again until your father gets home from work. Do you understand?"

I pressed my hand to my lips again, warning away the tears.

"Yes," I said very quietly.

"Then go to your room now."

I turned my back on her and ran to my room, holding the door open long enough for Mo-Mo to bolt through before slamming it as hard as I could. Then I threw myself down on my bed and began to sob. I cried in frustration and I cried in anger, because Kizzy had wandered away one summer morning, because my mother could not get past her fears, because Yeshi could fly halfway across the world but he couldn't get a stupid cell phone. Because if my mother had her way, I would never see Yeshi and Rinpoche again.

And because this was my fault. It was stupid and unfair and ridiculous, but it had happened because I did something my mother had told me not to do. And because of that, I could not tell my friends that they were in danger. I could not tell them that we had been right about the red-haired man. That he was a bad man. That he wanted the Tsiu Marpo statue and would do anything to get it.

I felt Mo-Mo's cool, damp nose nudging one of my hands. Then the bed shook as he jumped up next to me. I opened my eyes in surprise. Mo-Mo had never once tried to get on my bed, but now he was standing over me, his breath warm on my neck. He made a small whine and nudged me again, his soulful eyes locked on mine.

I understood him immediately.

It didn't matter if my motives were misunderstood, if I were labeled defiant or childish or vengeful. It didn't matter what punishment came down on me later. There was no room for "me" in this, there was no place for my ego. There were things happening on the mountain that were much bigger than me, much bigger than any one person. I knew what I had to do, and I knew there wasn't much time. I rubbed the tears from my face and sat up. I wrapped my arms around Mo-Mo's huge neck and pressed my face into his wild mane. I loved him so much in this moment, I thought my heart would break. But my heart was just another detail that had no part in the greater story.

I got up and moved quickly and quietly around the room, placing a few things in my pack and checking to make sure the flashlights were still there. I started to zip up the bag, then crossed to my bookcase. I grabbed three mystery novels and crammed them into the pack. I knew after that day, I really would never see Yeshi again. I wanted him to have the books I'd promised him.

There was no way to know how long it would be before my mother found the note. And I didn't have time to explain anyway. So I wrote simply,

There is something I have to do. When I am done, I will come home and take any punishment you give me. I am sorry.

Then I opened my window as far as it would go, and I pushed a chair under it.

"What do you think, boy? If you get on the chair, can you jump out of the window?"

Though he clearly understood what I wanted him to do, Mo-Mo had trouble getting his huge body onto the narrow window ledge. Finally, I made stirrups of my hands, and when his front paws were on the window ledge, I lifted his back paws. It required every ounce of strength I had, but suddenly the dog was gone, and when I leaned out the window, he was standing safely on the ground, waiting. I dropped my pack out first, then climbed after it, landing on the grass with a quiet thud. I pulled the window partway closed, strapped on my pack, and I was ready.

We ran together toward the path.

Chapter Eleven

Mo-Mo ran ahead of me, then circled back. He stayed next to me only for a few moments before he ran ahead again, and circled back once again. The blue patch of sky was completely gone, and the sky was heavy with dark clouds.

"I'm sorry," I said. "I'm going as fast as I can, honestly, and I've got extra stuff in my pack."

I checked my phone for the time — it was twelve thirty. I noticed with dismay that my battery wasn't fully charged. I should keep the phone powered off until I needed it. Before I did that, I stopped long enough to send a quick email to Dr. Bell. All it said was, "Hypothetical is now real. Taking your advice and using greatest possible caution." It was silly, but I felt I wanted at least one person in the world to know where I was going, and why.

I turned off the phone and zipped it back into my pack as the first few drops of rain fell. We climbed Lotus Trail in silence as the rain began falling more steadily. The wind began to pick up as well. By the time we'd turned onto the little path to the monastery, the sky was darkening to a grayish-green. The prayer flags were being whipped first in one direction, then another, blowing sideways, then upside-down in the chaos of the growing wind.

I knocked on the front door just as the rain began to fall in heavy sheets, and didn't wait for an answer. Once Mo-Mo and I were both safely in, I pushed the door closed and sighed with relief. The downpour had begun, and I was very grateful to have made it to the monastery without getting totally drenched. It was very dark inside. The door to the shrine room was closed. But I could see the glow of soft light coming from the kitchen, and something smelled delicious. Without hesitation, I followed my nose.

Yeshi was standing near the stove, peering into a pan that was set on a small gas-operated cooker on the counter. He turned when I came in, and his face lit up.

"You're here! I thought the weather would keep you away, but you came early to beat it. This is perfect timing, because I am making momos!"

I flushed with pleasure that Yeshi was so happy to see me, momentarily forgetting that I had come with dire warnings and fears for his safety.

"What's that thing you're cooking on?" I asked.

"Oh, it's a camping stove," Yeshi told me. "This kitchen stove won't work until we get electricity service, and we haven't done that yet."

"I can't believe you've been up here all this time with no electricity," I said.

Yeshi shrugged.

"It's no problem," he said. "As long as we get it in time for our reopening. Some other monks will be visiting to attend the celebration of the return of Rinpoche's teacher. It is better if we have electricity by then because of the guests."

"I'm still confused about that," I said, sitting at the table. Yeshi sat down too and began flattening a sheet of white dough with a roller. "You said Rinpoche's teacher died."

"Yes," he said, nodding. "In 1984."

"So . . . when you say that he's returned . . ."

Yeshi looked confused, then he smiled. "I have to remember you don't know all these things. You just seem like you belong here, Jax. Sometimes I forget you're not Tibetan. You seem like one, except for those blue eyes you have."

From everything I knew about Yeshi and Rinpoche, I knew this was the greatest of compliments.

But if Yeshi had seen me shouting at my mother this morning, he might not think so highly of me, I thought ruefully.

"There are teachers like the one Rinpoche built this monastery for, who are very wise, very advanced, who have ancient teachings that have been passed directly from one lama to the next for centuries. We call them *tulku*. When a *tulku* dies, he can choose when and where he will be reborn. His students will look for signs and seek divinations to give them clues to his whereabouts. Sometimes it takes months; sometimes it takes years. Search parties go out, following the clues until they have found the teacher with his new face. This is the way the teacher returns. He will go back to his monastery, and one day he will become the teacher again. And so it goes, cycle after cycle."

Suddenly, Yeshi laughed. "You should see your face!" he exclaimed.

I covered it with my hands for a moment. I guess my mouth had been gaping open.

"Sorry, no. I just . . . it's incredible. But I don't understand how. Or not how, but okay, so the *tulku* comes back, but now he's a baby. So is he, like . . . himself? In a baby body?"

Yeshi laughed, and I winced a little, feeling I had asked something stupid.

"It's a very good question. You know, these are things we study all of our lives and never completely understand. But no, the person is not the same person in a baby body. Okay, here is an example. Do you know who the Dalai Lama is?"

"Sure, he's the happy monk, he's like the . . . the top . . . the number one monk. . . ." My voice trailed off.

"He is, exactly. The Dalai Lama is the spiritual head of all Tibetans. Very wise, very enlightened. This Dalai Lama, the one whose face you know, the happy monk, his name is Tenzin Gyatso. He is the fourteenth Dalai Lama. When he was a small boy, and the thirteenth Dalai Lama died, search parties found him. And you know, he was a regular boy from a small village, but from then on, he is given all the teachings, all the knowledge the Dalai Lama must have. He has to learn everything again too. But it isn't that at some point he says, 'Oh, yes, I remember now that I was this other person before.' He may remember little things. But he is himself, a new person who contains the teacher who came before him, the thirteenth."

"It's kind of amazing," I said. "I actually really like the idea that a teacher returns over and over again to continue his work."

Yeshi nodded, using a jar lid to cut the flattened dough into little circles. "That is exactly right, Jax. How do you know so much, anyway?"

I sighed. "Well, speaking of stuff I know, I have more to tell you. And it's really important."

Yeshi looked up quickly. "Did you hear back from the museum people?" he asked eagerly.

"I actually did! And not only that, the email was from Thomas Bell himself — the person who was the assistant to the chief curator in that article we read. To be honest, this is the reason I rushed up here even with the storm coming."

I told him everything Thomas Bell had said, and then everything that happened with Kizzy and the red-haired man. Yeshi looked alarmed when I told him how the man had gotten angry and threatening, but I rushed to get it all out before he could say anything.

Finally, I took a deep breath and added, "I think you're in danger. I think you and Rinpoche are both in danger. This storm is supposed to be pretty intense for a while, and you don't have a car, so obviously we can't go anywhere right now. But I think we should at least call the police and let them know this man is out there. My cell phone battery is running low, but there's enough power for me to call them and explain."

"No, no police!" Yeshi said, with an intensity that surprised me.

"But . . . I mean, can I ask why not?"

Yeshi looked stricken.

"Police bring trouble," Yeshi said. "Rinpoche would not say it, but I will — I am afraid of them."

"But why? The police are here to help us, to protect us from bad guys."

Yeshi's eyes were down.

"Not in Tibet," he said quietly. "Police, state security, soldiers. They don't protect us. They bring trouble. They take monks away."

I didn't know what to say. There was so much I didn't know about Yeshi's life before he came here. I put a hand on his wrist.

"Yeshi, I won't do anything you don't want me to do. But here, where I live, the police are your friends. If they came here, it would only be to make sure you and Rinpoche are safe. And to stop anyone from stealing from you."

Yeshi looked up at me, his clear brown eyes filled with concern.

"If you say we should call them, Jax, I trust you. This is your country, and I know many things here are different."

I took a deep breath, remembering my mother saying that she trusted me this morning. I put the memory of that out of my mind and focused on Yeshi.

"Okay. I guess for right now, at this moment, there's no point in calling them, because nothing has actually happened yet. I guess we can't really call the police to say somebody might come and steal something, or hurt someone. But if something does happen, if we see him, then we should call."

Yeshi nodded. "Okay. That is what we will do."

He gave a heavy sigh, stacked the round discs of dough he had been making, then stood up and turned off the stove.

"And, hopefully, this storm will pass quickly and we can get you and Rinpoche out of here to somewhere safer. Someone with a truck or an SUV could drive up the old logging trail to get you."

"I know you are right, and we must keep Rinpoche safe. But, Jax, I don't want to think about what might happen if this man comes back and we are *not* here. Rinpoche cannot lose that statue. He must bring it back to Tibet. Did Thomas Bell know anything about the prophecy?"

"Oh, yes!" I said, pulling out my phone. "He actually sent me part of it. I have it on my phone. But I have to tell you, I can't make heads or tails of it."

"Read it to me," Yeshi requested.

"Okay. And maybe you can write some notes down while I'm reading? That way I can turn the phone off afterward and save power. In case we need to make a call later. I have a little pad and pen in my backpack."

Yeshi retrieved the notebook and pen as I powered up my phone and found the document Dr. Bell had sent.

The first rumble of thunder crackled over the mountain. It was very dark out now, even though it was the middle of the afternoon. Preparing to read the prophecy out loud in the monastery, the room lit mostly by candles, I felt a current of fear snake up my spine. What if by just reading it, I unleashed something?

Yeshi watched me expectantly. I took a deep breath, and read the excerpt Dr. Bell had sent.

"See what I mean?" I asked when I was done. "I mean, does any of that make sense?"

Yeshi continued writing for a few moments before answering.

"We need to look for a different kind of sense, Jax. An oracle wrote this. It isn't a newspaper article, where things are exactly what it says they are. It's more like remembering a strange dream, then realizing it has a meaning to you. Let's start with the beginning."

We looked down at the words on my phone, reading silently together.

Six snakes coil at the root of the black tree when ocean walkers plunder the snow caves and gompas *on the rooftop of the world.*

"The six snakes. That might be a measure of time," Yeshi said, making another note. "Like in sixty years or six hundred years or something. I don't know. And a *gompa* is a monastery. Ocean walker . . . someone who crossed the ocean? Came from another country far away to Tibet to steal things? Perhaps it means the red-haired man?"

I raised my eyebrows. "Wow. You really can understand this stuff."

Yeshi shook his head. "I'm only guessing. Okay, next."

With the last breath of the mountain abbot is lost the hidden word of the Lotus-born.

"The mountain abbot — Rinpoche's teacher spent many years living in a mountain cave and meditating alone. The mountain abbot could be Rinpoche's teacher. The Lotus-born is another name we call Padmasambhava, but I don't know what 'the hidden word' means," Yeshi mused.

I remembered something.

"Dr. Bell talked about Pommasa . . . the name you just said — and he told me Pamasum . . .

"Padmasambhava," Yeshi offered.

"Yes, that guy, that he hid secret teachings all over Tibet in all different kinds of places, including clues and messages that might be inside a statue!"

Yeshi drew a deep breath. "This statue holds a lost teaching of Padmasambhava? Then it is a priceless treasure — no wonder they sent Rinpoche halfway around the world to find it."

"This next bit gets weird," I said.

When the moon-marked boy rides the sky ship into the setting sun, a sleeping demon will stir. Then comes the protector to the innocent with eyes of lapis, and he shall be guardian and protector to this dakini, *and together they are as an army.*

"I mean, right? Can you make anything out of that?" I asked.

Yeshi looked like he was lost in thought for a moment. He wrote some more in the notebook. Then he seemed to hear me. He pushed the sleeve of his shirt up over his shoulder. He had a raised, red birthmark there in the shape of a perfect crescent.

"I think I am the moon-marked boy," Yeshi said quietly. "And I got on an airplane and traveled to the west. To America."

"Riding the sky ship into the setting sun," I said, amazed. "And the innocent with eyes of lapis? The *dakini* who the protector comes to guard? Who's that?"

Yeshi sat back in his chair and fixed me with an appraising look.

"Well, lapis is an important stone in Tibet — it is blue. Blue-eyed. And a *dakini* is a female protector. A blue-eyed female. You. And Mo-Mo would be the protector. Your protector."

I felt that the floor shifted suddenly, and I held on to the side of the chair. The room seemed to spin, and I felt I couldn't breathe. Me? In a two-hundred-year-old prophecy? It was one thing for Yeshi to talk about reincarnation, about search parties looking for Tibetan children with the memories of ancients. But this was me. I was . . . what? What was I?

"It sounds very strange to you, I know," Yeshi said. "But we're only taking these words and using them to help us understand what we need to do. These are clues, things meant to get us thinking in the right direction. Try not to think about it too literally, okay?"

I nodded.

Beneath a skyless void lies the treasure, and the hidden memory awaits in a door that clatters below twenty-eight feet. Shall the Rightful Teacher open the door, the demon Dharma protector shall slumber, but the hand of the Ocean Walker will ignite his wrath, and all the afflictions of the dark age will prosper, and the blood of the Precious One shall be spilled.

"A lot of this part . . . I don't really know," Yeshi said. "I'm not coming up with anything."

"Me neither," I said. "Except it seems to say that if this ocean walker, like one of those people who plundered relics from monasteries, takes the statue, it's going to be very, very bad."

"And the blood of the Precious One shall be spilled," Yeshi remembered.

"What does that mean?"

"If you translate *Precious One* into Tibetan, it is *Rinpoche*," Yeshi said very quietly.

Rinpoche.

A sudden, loud clattering sound erupted from the direction of the hall. Yeshi and I exchanged a quick look, then jumped up. I grabbed my phone in case I needed to place a quick call for help. Mo–Mo dashed in front of us, pausing to give me a brief reproachful look that said *I go first.*

Rinpoche was in the hallway, his robes billowing. A side-hinged window had blown open, and Rinpoche had stepped up onto the sill, wind and rain blowing in on him as he tried to push the window shut with his shoulder.

"Wait, let me help!" Yeshi cried.

Rinpoche called out something in Tibetan. Yeshi stepped up behind him and pushed both his hands against the window. Together, they were able to slam it closed, and Rinpoche slipped the latch into the locked position.

"Phew," Yeshi said. "It's really blowing out there."

Rinpoche turned as if he were getting ready to hop down off the windowsill, which was soaked with rain. But before he could balance himself, one foot slipped on the slick wood surface and he plummeted to the floor, hitting it hard with an ominous thud.

Chapter Twelve

"Are you sure?" I asked anxiously.

We had helped Rinpoche back into the shrine room, where he was sitting on a small, round cushion with his right leg propped up in front of him.

"Thank you, Jax-la," he said. "I am sure. This . . . cold bag?"

"Ice pack," Yeshi corrected.

"Yes, it is very good. Only thing I need."

"I always have an instant ice pack in my hiking bag in case I twist an ankle," I explained. "I have an Ace bandage too. After the swelling has gone down some, I can wrap it for you, to help you walk. If it isn't broken, that is."

Neither Yeshi nor Rinpoche responded. What if it was broken? I must have been crazy to march up here alone, thinking Yeshi and I could handle everything ourselves.

"Best for me just sitting quietly here," Rinpoche said, giving me a reassuring look. "Good place to be."

I looked around curiously. This was the first time I'd ever seen the shrine room. It was a large, rectangular room under a peaked roof, with two small windows along one wall and a raised area in the ceiling with a skylight. The walls were covered with silk hangings in yellows and blues and burgundies, and elaborate geometrically patterned borders framed each window. At one end of the room was a larger-than-life Buddha, painted gold save the top of his head, which was deep blue. Behind the Buddha were rows and rows of little dishes with candles burning in them. And overhead I noticed glassed-in cabinets that looked like bookshelves, behind which sat hundreds of statues of little Buddhas, lined up in row after row. There was a deep quiet feeling in the room, both an absence of sound and an absence of motion. The yellow flickering light from the candles and the smell of wood-scented incense made everything seem very dreamlike.

"It's time now," Yeshi said to me. I didn't need him to explain what he meant. We had to tell Rinpoche what we knew. We had to tell him everything.

Yeshi did most of the talking in Tibetan, with me adding details about the red-haired man and my email exchange with Dr. Bell. Rinpoche said something I couldn't understand, and Yeshi exclaimed with surprise.

"Rinpoche says he knows Thomas Bell," he told me excitedly. "He says he remembers the English researchers who came to his monastery to study the statue, and Dr. Bell was a young assistant with them, and the only one who could speak Tibetan. He says he is a good man, and he has given you good advice."

"Wow," I said. I wondered silently why Dr. Bell would not have told me he knew Rinpoche. Then I remembered what Yeshi had told me — that Rinpoche was a title of respect given to certain teachers who had returned through reincarnation to continue teaching. So it could be any of a number of people.

Rinpoche was speaking again, and Yeshi shaking his head.

"No, we didn't look inside all the crates yet," he answered in English. "I think we saw half, maybe more."

"Now is good to look," Rinpoche told us. "If the Ocean Walker will come soon, we must find the statue before."

"Yes, Rinpoche," Yeshi said, standing up.

"Will you be okay here by yourself?" I asked.

Rinpoche smiled.

"Yes. I am where I should be," he told me, his bright, clear gaze fixed on me.

"We'll work fast," Yeshi promised.

Once again, Mo-Mo circled in front of us and went out ahead. Yeshi pulled the shrine room door closed behind him. The wind was really howling now — the kind of wind that brought big trees down. Fortunately, there weren't any directly over the monastery. *The prayer flags would be ripped to shreds, though,* I thought sadly.

My backpack was still in the kitchen, the contents spilled onto the table from when I dumped it out, looking for the instant ice compress. I picked up the electric lanterns and handed one to Yeshi. He removed the wall hanging and slid the little table away from the basement door. I opened it, and Mo-Mo slipped by, hesitating for a moment at the top of the stairs. I held the lantern out to illuminate the way down as best I could, and Mo-Mo went down the steps, with Yeshi and I following him like baby ducklings.

The chamber looked untouched, just as we had left it, every crate carefully closed and replaced. Mo-Mo sat at the foot of the stairs, where he could both watch us and keep an eye on the kitchen doorway.

"I think we had gotten to this one," I said, pointing at a crate toward the back of the chamber.

"That's right," Yeshi said. He pried the lid off and sifted through the contents. He pulled out several small clay figures of little Buddhas.

"Statues!" I exclaimed.

"*Tsa tsas*," he said. "These are a kind of small clay statue, not what we are looking for."

He placed them gently back in the crate and pulled it onto the floor without reclosing it.

"We'll have to put everything back later," he said. "No time now."

"Maybe we should both be opening crates so we can go through them faster," I said.

Yeshi nodded. "Good idea."

We worked quickly and quietly. I pulled the top off the small crate closest to me. Inside was a wall hanging similar to the one that covered the kitchen door, containing a painting of a seated figure with four arms. But the painting was damaged — I could see part of a cloud behind the figure's head, but the rest had been ripped away. I sifted through the crate quickly, but the top half of the painting wasn't there. I put the torn painting back and set the crate aside, and was opening the next one, when Mo-Mo began growling. Yeshi and I both froze, then Yeshi lifted his lantern up so the light spilled over the enormous dog. He was staring intently at the kitchen door, his hackles raised, and his teeth bared in a snarl. My heart began to race.

"What is it?" I whispered.

"I don't know," Yeshi said, not quite hiding the tremor in his voice. "But something's not right, and Rinpoche is up there alone. We'd better go."

I followed Yeshi to the bottom of the stairs, and Mo-Mo shot up them. I reached into my back pocket for my phone. It wasn't there! I racked my brain. I had been sitting on the floor in the monastery room when I put the ice pack on Rinpoche's knee. I would have taken it out of my pocket then. Was it still there, on the floor?

"Jax, come on!" Yeshi called down the stairs anxiously. Mo-Mo was waiting next to him in the kitchen. As soon as I came through the door into the kitchen, Mo-Mo headed straight down the hallway, stopping when he came to the monastery entrance. He began to bark — a deep, booming sound that echoed off the walls like thunder.

I ran to the window — the one that had blown open earlier. It was hard to see anything outside, the sky was so dark and sheets of heavy rain were blowing almost sideways. But then I glimpsed something, a splash of color in the woods. Someone was out there, heading for the monastery. I opened my mouth to tell Yeshi, but the words caught in my mouth when I saw a second figure emerge from the woods. The Ocean Walker was coming for his treasure, and this time he'd brought help.

"Two of them!" I whispered.

Instantly, Yeshi dashed to the door and slid the bolt into place. Then he pointed to the shrine room.

"In there," he whispered.

"Mo-Mo, come!" I hissed.

Mo-Mo barked again at the door, then he turned and came to me.

We slipped into the shrine room, where Rinpoche was sitting just where we'd left him, nodding as if he'd been expecting us.

"The Ocean Walker," he said, though he couldn't possibly have known that.

"And he brought someone else," Yeshi said. "I'm sorry, Rinpoche. We didn't find the statue."

"The night is long," Rinpoche said, almost conversationally.

I began to look for my phone. But the shrine room was only dimly lit, and there were little meditation cushions all over the floor. I picked cushions up, looking beneath them or behind them. No phone.

The sound of pounding erupted, fists hammering on wood. Yeshi's face was tight with fear, but Rinpoche merely looked up, curiously. After several moments, we heard the sound of shattering glass. Mo-Mo bared his teeth again but fell completely silent.

"They're coming inside," Yeshi whispered. "Is this a good time to call the police, Jax?"

My eyes filled with tears. "I can't find my phone," I told him. "I think it might be in here somewhere, but I don't see it. I'm so sorry!"

"It's okay," Yeshi said. "The Ocean Walker is here now. There is no time for help to come."

A feeling of dread filled me. What had I gotten myself into? I wished I'd never set eyes on the horrible Ocean Walker. But I didn't regret my decision to come to the monastery today. Whatever happened, I would know I'd tried — I had done my best to warn them and try to keep them safe. I'd done some things right, and some things wrong, like losing my phone. Seriously? Though Yeshi was right — even if I had called them, the police could not get up this road and find the monastery immediately. And Mo-Mo was doing his best to protect us, and he would keep on protecting us as long as he could.

The shrine room door flew open with a bang. The red-haired man I now thought of as the Ocean Walker came in, followed by an enormous guy with a pocked face and a crew cut and dull, angry eyes. I looked at Rinpoche, who was watching the men calmly. I don't know why he wasn't afraid. But I did know that he was a special teacher, that he understood the world in a way most people could never imagine. Somehow, that helped me feel better. But still, I was scared.

Mo-Mo stood up and raised his head, issuing a menacing snarl. The heavyset man picked up a painted table sitting near the back of the shrine room and smashed it onto the ground. He picked up one of the broken table's heavy wooden legs and held it out like a club.

"Call him off, or the next step he takes will be his last one," ordered the Ocean Walker.

"Mo-Mo, down," I said. My faithful dog obeyed instantly and fell silent, his eyes fixed on the intruders.

"Now, I got my hands on some very interesting blueprints. There's a chamber below this monastery that isn't listed in the building plan. The access point to that chamber is a room on the eastern side of the building. There are boxes stored down there — they were put there in 1984 and left. One of those boxes contains the artifact I'm looking for. Don't bother arguing. I know all about it. You kids, both of you — take me down there now. Walter, you stay here and guard the old guy and the dog. And if that animal makes so much as a move, smash it on the head."

"Don't hurt him!" I cried.

"You all do exactly what I say, and nobody has to get hurt."

I didn't believe him. I don't think any of us did, but Yeshi and I stood up to go with him.

"Stay with Rinpoche, Mo-Mo," I said.

Mo-Mo didn't move, but he stared up at me with huge, sad eyes.

"Move," said the man. "Any problems, Walter, you just holler."

Walter nodded and stood, holding his club not too far from Rinpoche's head. Rinpoche, who looked almost serene in the flickering candlelight, ignored Walter completely. The man might have been holding a bouquet of flowers, the way Rinpoche was acting.

"Just hurry it up," Walter said. "This place gives me the creeps."

Yeshi and I left the room, exchanging a worried look.

A loud clap of thunder exploded outside, followed by a flash of lightning.

No one spoke as we walked to the kitchen, picked up the lanterns we'd left there, and descended into the room below. The Ocean Walker grabbed Yeshi's lantern and held it up, looking around the room. He whistled when he saw all the crates.

"I knew it," he said. "You two, over here."

We walked to the space beneath the staircase where he was pointing. Pulling a length of blue nylon cord from his pocket, he wrapped Yeshi's wrist, then mine, then tied the other end around the wooden beam supporting the underside of the steps.

"Where is it?" he demanded, shining the light directly in my face.

"I don't know," I told him.

"That's not what you said this morning," he sneered. "You said you knew exactly where it was. And you better not have been lying. You're going to tell me what you know, or I'm going to tell Walter to get it out of the old man."

"He doesn't know anything!" I cried.

"Well, you better hope I find something in one of these boxes, or I'm going to have to go question your old friend myself."

He put one lantern on the steps and left the other near his feet. As I watched in dismay, he began tearing into the crates like a greedy child in a candy shop. He opened the first one and pulled out the black lacquered music box. He took one look at it and cast it aside. When it hit the ground, it smashed into small pieces. He went through every crate that way, grabbing the contents, then hurling them aside, picking up the smaller boxes and dumping them onto the floor, then kicking the objects aside. I bit my lip, tears springing to my eyes. All of the Mountain Abbot's gifts were being tossed aside, stomped underfoot like garbage. What kind of delusional greed could drive a person to this?

As he continued his rampage, I could feel Yeshi making small movements with his hand, trying to slip free. I positioned myself slightly in front of him, so that if the Ocean Walker looked suddenly in our direction, he wouldn't see what Yeshi was doing.

I watched as the man pulled the tops off the last remaining crates, exclaiming in disgust as he pulled the torn painting from the crate, then flung it back in. He whirled around and walked toward me.

"You know something," he said. "And you're going to tell me what it is right now. Because if you don't, I'm gonna go find your red-robed buddy up there, and I'm going to do whatever I have to until he tells me something I want to know. Understand?"

I could see his dark, cold eyes in the lantern light. *His soul is dead,* I thought. And I remembered the prophecy:

The blood of the Precious One shall be spilled. I knew the Ocean Walker was perfectly capable of carrying out his threat. I didn't want to do anything to help this monster find the statue. But I couldn't let him hurt Rinpoche. I heard Rinpoche's voice in my head: *The night is long.* I had to buy us some time. But I didn't know anything else. The words of the prophecy jumbled through my mind. Twenty-eight feet. Beneath the skyless void. Hidden words.

Skyless void. Those words stuck in my head. Where had I seen something with no sky?

"There's a crate with a torn painting in it," I said quickly.

"I saw it," he said. "It's just an old worthless *thangka* torn in two."

And the top half was missing. There was no sky.

Beneath the skyless void.

"There's something under it," I said. Behind me, I felt the rope fall slack. Yeshi was free, and now the rope hung only loosely on my own wrist. Had the Ocean Walker noticed?

He hadn't, because he was already racing back to the crate, which he grabbed and carried to the steps where he'd placed the second lantern. He threw the *thangka* on the ground and eagerly pulled out the rest of the wrapping. Then he glared at me.

"There's nothing here!"

"There is," I insisted. "Maybe there's a compartment. Maybe something is taped to the bottom."

He slammed the crate against the ground and kicked it, then exclaimed.

"What the —." He stopped speaking as he pulled a piece of flat wood up and out of the crate. *A false bottom,* I thought. I had been right — I had figured out part of the prophecy. But it was too late.

The Ocean Walker shined the light into the crate.

"My God," he whispered. "There it is."

As he reached for something at the bottom of the crate, I felt Yeshi slip past me.

"Leave it alone!" Yeshi shouted, rushing the man as though he meant to tackle him.

"Yeshi, don't!" I yelled, but the Ocean Walker had jumped up with a snarl as Yeshi charged, raising his lantern with both hands to slam it into Yeshi's head.

I screamed and closed my eyes. I heard a loud smack, and the thud of a body hitting the ground. I couldn't bear to look. I just stood there with my face covered, waiting for the Ocean Walker to do the same thing to me.

"I'm okay," I heard Yeshi say very quietly, as if he didn't quite believe it.

I took my hands away from my face and opened my eyes. Yeshi was standing there, unharmed, the Ocean Walker in a crumpled heap at the foot of the stairs. A light was shining from the stairs. Someone was standing there, only a shadow behind the beam of a large, powerful flashlight. Confused, I stepped past Yeshi and looked up the stairs, into the face of a white-haired man I'd never seen before, holding a heavy wood cane in one hand.

I took one step toward him, moving into the beam of his light.

"Jax?" the man asked.

I was too astonished to speak, so I just nodded dumbly.

"I'm Dr. Bell. Thomas Bell. I've come to help."

Chapter Thirteen

"I'll explain later," Dr. Bell said. "But the moment I read your email today, I jumped into my car and headed here. I would have come sooner, but my car got stuck on the logging road. I had to walk the rest of the way. Where is Rinpoche?"

"In the shrine room," Yeshi said anxiously. "Another man is guarding him."

"We'd better get up there, then," Dr. Bell said. "I don't think this one's going anywhere for a while. I gave him a pretty good whack on the head. Come on."

Dr. Bell bent over and picked up the Ocean Walker's lantern where it had fallen on the step. He held it gingerly and distastefully away from his body, as if it were a snake.

"Right. Let's see about Rinpoche," he said, in a crisp British accent.

Yeshi went up first, followed by the doctor. Before going up, I leaned over the crate and saw an object tightly packed into the base, wrapped in yellow silk. I took it in my hands, surprised at its weight. The silk was disintegrating in my hands, the face of the demon clearly visible.

I hope Tsiu Marpo knows I'm only bringing this to Rinpoche and not trying to steal it, I thought nervously, negotiating each step carefully.

Dr. Bell popped back into the doorway just as I reached it.

"Coming?" he asked.

"I just had to get this," I said, nodding at the bundle in my hands.

His eyes widened as he saw the half-wrapped statue.

"Please, we have to hurry!" Yeshi whispered.

Dr. Bell nodded, setting off down the hall as quickly and silently as a cat. Even his cane seemed to make no sound when it touched the floor. As we moved, I tucked the statue under my arm. Was it too convenient, Dr. Bell showing up the very moment the Ocean Walker found the statue? Maybe I'd been too trusting, told him too much. But if he was a bad guy, why would Dr. Bell have shared everything he knew with me? Why would he have given me the prophecy and warned me about the Ocean Walker? *Mo-Mo will know,* I thought suddenly. *If Dr. Bell means me harm or intends to steal the statue, Mo-Mo will attack him.*

Rinpoche and Mo-Mo hadn't moved. Walter jumped to his feet when he saw us, and held the club high in the air, first brandishing it at us, then moving to stand behind Rinpoche, showing us he could bring the heavy piece of wood down on the monk's head at any moment. I lingered in the doorway, unsure what to do, now clutching the statue in both hands. Mo-Mo made no move to threaten Dr. Bell. He kept his focus on Walter.

"Put that cane on the floor," Walter commanded.

Dr. Bell looked surprised, as if he'd forgotten it was anything but a walking aid.

"I'm afraid I'll get a bit doddery on my legs if I do that," he replied, and for a moment, I thought I was going to burst out laughing, his statement was so polite and absurd.

"Put it down," Walter shouted.

"As long as you put that wooden club down first," he insisted. Then he added, "Rinpoche-la, *deer nga-tsor koo-nyen yö.*"

Dr. Bell spoke Tibetan, and addressed Rinpoche with the *la* added for affection. He wasn't an enemy after all. Rinpoche smiled and nodded. Then he closed his eyes and began to throat sing.

"What's he doing? Tell him to stop," Walter said. The eerie and beautiful sound coming from Rinpoche only deepened and grew louder, bouncing off the shrine walls. Mo-Mo threw his head back and howled like a wolf. It was then I noticed that the statue seemed to be growing warmer in my hands. At that same moment I was feeling the strange heat through my fingers, I heard a distinctive third voice join those of Rinpoche and Mo-Mo, almost as if someone had chimed in harmony to create a three-note chord. Three voices, but only two singers. Who, or what, had joined in?

"Stop all this mumbo jumbo stuff!" yelled Walter, who was looking around wildly, probably wondering what had happened to the Ocean Walker.

He's really scared, I thought. *He's been scared of this place since he got here.*

"You've awakened a curse by threatening Rinpoche," I said. "You better get out of here while there's still time. Haven't you ever heard what happens to people who threaten violence in a Buddhist temple?"

"Shut up!" Walter yelled. But he was backing away from Rinpoche, lowering the club.

It's working, I thought. *Pile it on.*

"Didn't your boss tell you about the thing you came here to steal? It's an ancient relic, a powerful statue of the demon Tsiu Marpo. And now you've awakened it, and the demon is coming to take his revenge!"

"She's right," said Dr. Bell, picking up on my tactic. "And I took the liberty of calling the police before I got here, so they'll be well on their way by now. But Tsiu Marpo will most likely have torn you to pieces before they arrive."

"You're all crazy! Nobody said anything about stealing relics, or demons, or nothing. I was only supposed to keep this old guy from leaving. I'm not getting paid enough to get mixed up in this!" yelled Walter. He dropped the club to the floor with a clatter and ran past me. I heard him unlock the main door and fling it open.

I turned toward Yeshi, my face shining. Rinpoche was still chanting. The sound of three voices still sang through the room, and the statue in my hands was as hot as a baked potato just out of the oven. I stood listening, amazed at the sound. Rinpoche's eyes were closed — did he even know Walter had left?

"He's gone!" I exclaimed. "We did it! We —"

The breath went out of me all at once as something slammed into me from behind. I was staggering off balance when someone grabbed my arms, and I felt the statue being ripped from my hands.

"No!" I yelled, as the Ocean Walker held up the statue of Tsiu Marpo triumphantly. Mo-Mo stopped howling and sprang toward the Ocean Walker, his teeth bared.

What happened next is still a blur. I saw Mo-Mo charging like an enraged grizzly bear. Saw the Ocean Walker rear back and hurl the heavy statue at the dog's head just as the room was filled with the brilliant flash of a lightning strike very close outside. As I heard Mo-Mo yelp in pain, a violent gust of wind rushed through the room, and the candles burning all around the shrine room blew out. The room was left in only dim illumination from the small windows. Figures seemed to be converging toward the center of the room, the Ocean Walker and Mo-Mo and I don't know who else. Or what else. The dark room erupted in a cacophony of sound that came from all directions at once. I struggled to identify it, then realized with a sense of dread what it was — the clattering of horses' hooves.

Tsiu Marpo had come.

I had never felt such terror in my life. I wanted to run, or drop to the floor and cover my eyes. I did not want to see a demon. I did not want a demon to see *me*.

But Yeshi had said he was a demon protector. That he had been tamed. Tsiu Marpo was dangerous only to enemies of the moon-marked boy and the lapis-eyed *dakini* and the Precious One.

The Ocean Walker had found Walter's club. He grabbed Rinpoche roughly by one arm, yanking him to his feet and brandishing the club high over his head. Dr. Bell ran toward them to help, but froze when it became clear the Ocean Walker could and would bring the club down on Rinpoche's skull. Dr. Bell raised his hands and held them, palms out.

"You don't want to do this," he said. "No one's been hurt yet — let the monk go."

"Give me the statue, old man!" the Ocean Walker growled.

"He doesn't speak English," Dr. Bell pleaded.

"Then you tell him to give it to me! I'll bust his head open if I have to!"

The sight of this vile man threatening Rinpoche drove all the fear I felt straight out of me. Rinpoche was trying to stay standing, but his bad ankle wouldn't hold him. When he began to fall forward, the Ocean Walker yanked him upright again. I practically exploded with rage at the sight.

"Tsiu Marpo!" I shouted. "This Ocean Walker plundered the snow caves of precious relics! He is stealing the hidden word of the Lotus-born! This Ocean Walker threatens to spill the blood of the Precious One!"

The Ocean Walker locked his arm around Rinpoche's neck and tried to get closer to me, but Mo-Mo lunged between us, snarling viciously.

"Tsiu Marpo, protect the hidden word and the Precious One! Do not let this Ocean Walker spill blood as the prophecy warns!" I cried.

"All right — I warned you," the Ocean Walker yelled, his face cold and his eyes dead with rage. He pushed Rinpoche back and lifted the club up high in the air with both hands.

"No!" screamed Yeshi, running at him. The Ocean Walker stopped long enough to aim a powerful kick at Yeshi, who fell backward, hitting the ground hard. Mo-Mo bounded to Yeshi's side. The Ocean Walker turned back and stepped toward Rinpoche, who simply stood there watching him.

"Say good-bye, monk," the Ocean Walker hissed, reaching for Rinpoche's robes with one hand. Mo-Mo snarled and sank his teeth into the man's pant leg.

As he tried to yank his leg free, the room went suddenly still, then a breeze of icy cold seemed to blast from all directions. I heard a loud, low sound that was like throat chanting, but deeper, louder. As a long, narrow horn was being sounded, the floor beneath my feet seemed to vibrate with it.

Suddenly, the Ocean Walker reared and shrieked, staggering backward, dropping the club and throwing his arms up in front of his face. Mo-Mo stayed right on him, crouched and snarling, ready to spring if he came at anyone again.

"Get it off! It's biting, it's choking me!" he screamed. "Get if *off*! *Help me!*"

He was still yelling and punching at the air with his arms when he staggered past me, stumbling as if something were grabbing him from behind. The sound of his yells continued, growing fainter as he lurched out of the shrine room, Mo-Mo still at his ankles, pouncing and snarling and urging him forward. The sounds eventually disappeared altogether, swallowed by the wind outside.

There was a momentary stunned silence in the room. Then Dr. Bell switched on his large flashlight. The statue was lying on the floor in the center of the room. Yeshi was crouching next to Rinpoche, who had sunk back to the floor, his hands protectively on the old monk's shoulders.

Dr. Bell picked up the statue, walked over to the old monk, and placed it in his hands.

Rinpoche held the artifact reverently, his face filled with emotion, tears streaming down his weathered cheeks.

"*Lha gyalo!*" he exclaimed.

"*Lha gyalo,*" Dr. Bell repeated. "The gods are victorious."

"Jax, you did it!" Yeshi exclaimed. "You summoned Tsiu Marpo! You summoned him and he came, and he drove the Ocean Walker out. You saved the statue, you saved Rinpoche!"

"Maybe I helped," I said. "But so did you. You charged the Ocean Walker. Dr. Bell tried to stop him too. And Mo-Mo had him by the leg! He did much more than I did."

I looked around, surprised he hadn't trotted over to me when he heard his name.

Mo-Mo was not in the shrine room.

"Where is he?" I asked, fear rising in my throat.

"Come on, we'll look," Yeshi said. "Dr. Bell, can you help Rinpoche? He needs to put his ankle up. We need another ice pack."

"Of course," Dr. Bell said. He kneeled next to Rinpoche and spoke quietly to him in Tibetan. I felt terrible that I'd ever suspected him of being another Ocean Walker, even if it was only for a few moments.

Yeshi and I ran through the monastery, checking every room, even the chamber below the kitchen. Mo-Mo was nowhere to be found.

I went out onto the front steps, yelling Mo-Mo's name into the gloom. The wind seemed to throw the thin sound of my voice right back at me. The rain had let up, but I could see no sign of my dog anywhere.

"Where is he?" I asked, pressing my hand over my mouth.

"I think he must have chased the Ocean Walker when he ran out," Yeshi said. "Mo-Mo knows he tried to hurt all of us. He wouldn't let him just escape. I think he must have followed him."

"Or he's hurt and bleeding somewhere in the rain," I said.

"He could be hurt," Yeshi said. "But remember the prophecy. Mo-Mo is the protector. And as long as the Ocean Walker is out on the mountain, you still need to be protected. Come back inside. Trust Mo-Mo to do what he came here to do."

I hesitated for a moment, staring out. The storm was beginning to let up, and it was lighter now. But I couldn't see any trace of Mo-Mo, nor could I hear him bark when I listened. I heard only the wind gusting through the trees.

"Jax," Yeshi said softly. "Let's go back inside to Rinpoche."

I wiped the tears from my eyes, turned, and went back into the monastery.

Chapter Fourteen

Yeshi was walking around the shrine room, relighting candles. Dr. Bell was sitting on the floor next to Rinpoche, both of their heads bent over the statue Rinpoche held in his hands. When he saw me, Dr. Bell stood up and came over to me.

"Are you all right?" he asked.

I nodded. There didn't seem to be any point in mentioning Mo-Mo.

"You've had rather a remarkable day," Dr. Bell said, his face breaking into a smile. He had a very short, white beard that matched his messy hair, and deep smile lines around his dark brown eyes. I liked the clipped, British way he spoke.

"It doesn't seem real," I said. "It all happened so fast."

Dr. Bell nodded gravely.

"After your first email, I did a bit of detective work," he told me. "I realized that Tangyeling Monastery was quite close to where you said you lived, and a Tibetan friend confirmed what I suspected — that my old friend

Jampa Rinpoche had recently traveled to Tangyeling to reopen the monastery for the return of his teacher. I told you no one knew what had become of the Tsiu Marpo statue, which is true.

"But I had my own theory, which was that it had been transported out of Tibet with a number of other items where it could remain essentially hidden in plain sight. One possibility would have been to include it with the many packages being sent from all over the world to Tangyeling Monastery, right here. When you began asking questions about that very statue, I knew it wasn't a coincidence. I would have come anyway, to see the monastery and to see Jampa Rinpoche again — I thought it a rare bit of luck we were both in America at the same time. The university where I'm visiting is only a few hours from here. But when I got your second email today, I suddenly felt it imperative that I get to the monastery straightaway."

"Did you really call the police before you came?" I asked hopefully, thinking of the Ocean Walker out on the mountain somewhere, escaping. The other one, Walter, I wasn't so worried about. He didn't seem to know what the Ocean Walker meant to do — he was more like a thug for hire.

"Yes, I did, although I'm afraid my story may have sounded rather far-fetched to them. They assured me they would send someone up to check on the monastery as soon as they could, but they had a limited number of patrol cars, and would have to handle accidents and storm-related emergencies first."

I laughed. "Yeah, we're a pretty small town, so there aren't that many police. But if they said they'd get here, they'll get here."

"So we'll sit tight and wait for the time being. That's perfectly fine with me, because I'd like to have a better look at that statue. Wouldn't you?"

"I just need to let my mother know I'm safe first," I said. "To make a very long story short, I was grounded today and I had to sneak out to get here. So not only is she worried, she's probably going to be furious with me."

"Oh, dear," he said. "Yes, of course. I'll wait. After all, it's because of you we've got the statue. You ought to be part of solving the last bit of this puzzle."

"Um, there's only one problem. I lost my phone in here somewhere. At least I think it was in here. Is yours still working?"

"I believe so," he replied, pulling it from his shirt pocket and handing it to me.

"Oh, your battery is really low too," I said. "I'll just send a text — that will take less juice."

I was secretly relieved. I had to let my mother know I was safe. She'd already had a bad scare today, and it pained me to think I had caused her to worry about me when I ran off. But texting meant I wouldn't actually have to talk to her, hear the fear and tears in her voice. I typed quickly.

> Mom, I am okay, don't worry. I lost my phone, so I'm using this one. I am at the monastery. It was super important I come here. Someone tried to break in to rob it. I need to wait until the police come so I can give them a statement. Then I promise to get a ride home. I know you are mad at me. I am so sorry.

"Thanks," I said, giving Dr. Bell back his phone.

"Of course. Ready to have a look at our Tsiu Marpo?"

"I . . . um, is it safe?" I asked, feeling a little foolish. But Dr. Bell simply nodded.

"Rinpoche has chanted a prayer of protection. It's quite safe," he assured me.

I wanted to ask what he thought had happened to the Ocean Walker, who had been screaming for us to get "it" off him, that he was being bitten and choked. Was he only confused in the dark and actually feeling Mo-Mo attack him? That seemed the most likely explanation, though a dog couldn't choke a person. And what about the fact that the statue grew hot in my hands? What about the sound of horses' hooves? Was I the only one who'd heard it?

Yeshi was sitting on the floor next to Rinpoche.

"Jax, come see," he called, patting the floor next to him.

Dr. Bell and I each took one of the round cushions like the ones Rinpoche and Yeshi were sitting on. Soon we were all seated, completing a small circle, the statue on the floor in the center.

"It's spectacular," Dr. Bell said softly. "I didn't dare dream I'd ever lay eyes on it again."

"I will bring it back to monastery; it will be well," Rinpoche said. "So now, now we must find *terma* or his power can be . . . moved?"

"Stolen," Yeshi corrected.

"Yes, stolen. Stolen other time, many times tomorrow."

"Then there really is a teaching of Pomsambeewa hidden somewhere on the statue?" I asked.

"Padmasambhava," Yeshi whispered, with a tiny wink. Darn. I actually thought I had almost sort of gotten close to getting it right that time.

"Not exactly," Dr. Bell said. "Most likely this *terma* we are looking for is more a code. Something we would call a *dakini* script. A clue, or perhaps a mental text."

"A mental text?" I asked.

"It's . . . oh, how do I put this? . . . A *dakini* script is somewhat like a coded message, written for the eyes of a treasure revealer. Others might be able to see writing, but to most, it would just look like nonsense — Tibetan-looking characters that aren't actually words. When the right person finds and reads the *dakini* script, it unlocks the code."

"What will it say?" I asked.

"It could be one of many things," Dr. Bell said. "Perhaps the location of a teaching in a cave or masked beneath a painting, or it may unlock the memory of a teaching that has been handed down from Rinpoche to Rinpoche. So we may be talking about a scroll buried away somewhere, but we can't assume that. The teaching could be right here, hidden in the memory of Rinpoche in all his successive past lives. Does that make any sense?"

"I don't know," I said truthfully. "But you mean we're looking for a message that's on the statue that Rinpoche will understand?"

"I will understand message, yes," Rinpoche said.

"What did the prophecy say about how the teaching was hidden?" Yeshi asked. "Jax?"

"Me?"

Everyone seemed to be looking at me. I closed my eyes for a moment, until the words came back into my head.

"The hidden memory awaits in a door that clatters below twenty-eight feet," I recited. I picked up the statue carefully, and turned it over. The bottom of the base was smooth, the surface uninterrupted.

"Could the measurement have translated wrong? Twenty-eight inches? Centimeters? Either way, there doesn't seem to be any place something could have been put inside this," I said. "It looks totally solid."

"Looks can be very deceiving," Dr. Bell said. "We've had pieces at the museum that appeared completely solid, yet when we X-ray them, we find that a relic has been placed inside."

"A horse's hooves clatter," Yeshi says. "Those are feet. But Tsiu Marpo's horse has only four feet."

"But didn't you tell me something about six demons that rode with Tsiu Marpo?" I asked.

Yeshi nodded, and Dr. Bell looked surprised.

"Yes, that's quite right — six Might Demons were born from his body," Dr. Bell said. "There are descriptions of all seven of them riding together. Seven horses times four feet. Twenty-eight feet. I think you're onto something, Jax!"

I swallowed the wave of pride I felt. Figuring out a bit of math wasn't going to find the hidden *terma*. I put the statue down on the floor, and ran my hands around the hooves of Tsiu Marpo's horse. Three of the hooves were flat on the base, but the right front hoof was raised slightly. I ran my finger around the outside of the raised hoof, and felt a tiny seam where the hoof met the beginning of the horse's leg. I wiggled it, and pulled on it, then tried doing both at the same time. Suddenly, the hoof popped open like a door on an invisible hinge.

I heard Yeshi draw in a quick breath. No one said anything. No one moved.

"Jax, may I?" Dr. Bell said quietly, after a long moment.

I handed the statue to him quickly. Frankly, just holding it kind of scared me. I knew it was okay now, with Rinpoche here and the Ocean Walker gone. But I still didn't like to have the statue in my hands, or even near me. A demon was a demon, after all, even if he'd been tamed.

Dr. Bell held the statue up and peered into the passage that lay behind the hoof. He put the statue down on its side, and reached into his pocket, pulling out a small case containing several tiny tools.

"Eyeglass repair kit," he explained. "I'm afraid I'm rather hard on my glasses — I never know when I might need to fix them. This ought to do quite nicely."

He pulled a magnifying glass and a tiny screwdriver from the case, now placing the statue upside-down on his lap. He made a few small, careful movements as if he were performing delicate surgery. My eyes widened when I saw him gently pull a tiny rolled-up piece of parchment from the hollow leg.

"Lha gyalo!" exclaimed Rinpoche.

Dr. Bell leaned forward and placed the little scroll in Rinpoche's hand. Rinpoche placed the unopened scroll in his lap, closed his eyes, and began to chant in Tibetan.

"Is he going to read it?" I whispered.

"He has to say many prayers first, many meditations," Yeshi said. "He will not read it until he is prepared."

Dr. Bell nodded.

"We should leave him be," Dr. Bell said quietly. "This part of the journey Jampa Rinpoche must make on his own."

We stood up and walked quietly from the room. Yeshi gently closed the door behind us.

"Come to the kitchen," Yeshi said. "I was going to make momos earlier. We can have them now, while we wait for the police."

The coziness of the kitchen was marred by the open door and the now dark staircase on the other side. I pulled the door shut, and replaced the table and the *thangka*. As if I'd flicked a switch, the kitchen seemed to be larger and lighter, and friendly.

"Oh, I haven't had a good momo in ages," Dr. Bell said, looking longingly at the little pile of round dough wrappers Yeshi had left on the table.

"I make great momos," Yeshi boasted. "But we have to work first and enjoy later."

Dr. Bell laughed. "I know how to do my part, I assure you. If you've an extra knife, I'll start dicing the onion and garlic while you do that cabbage. This is the easy bit. I've never quite had the knack for making them into dumplings. Mine always fall apart, and the insides dump out."

They worked together like a couple of old friends. Dr. Bell seemed to know exactly what was supposed to be chopped up, and how much. They didn't ask me to help, and I was glad. As my mother often pointed out, the only thing I could do in the kitchen was boil an egg, and I sometimes managed to mess up even that.

"And what do you think of Tangyeling, Yeshi-la?" Dr. Bell asked.

"I think it's perfect," Yeshi declared. "We arrived on the mountain after the sun had gone down. When I woke up the next morning and looked outside, I couldn't believe it. I said to Rinpoche, 'We are back in Tibet!'"

"It looks like Tibet here?" I asked, amazed.

"Oh, yes," Yeshi said. "Where I am from, we live on a mountain just like this, but higher. Everything is surrounded by trees and little streams going right up the slope, so high you get to the place where the trees won't grow anymore. Then it's all snow and rocks to the very top. In Tibet, Buddhism came first to our mountains, so they are sacred to us."

"You really miss it, don't you?" I said.

Yeshi nodded.

"I do too," Dr. Bell said. "It's been a long time since I've been there. It's too difficult to travel into Tibet now. I fear I may never get there again. But this is a happy occasion. Will there be many guests for the ceremony?"

"Ceremony?" I asked.

"For the official reopening of the monastery," Dr. Bell explained. "And the celebration welcoming the return of Jampa's teacher."

I'd almost forgotten about that, with all the Ocean Walker drama. I was extremely curious to see the teacher, but I also dreaded the prospect, because once he arrived and took his place at Tangyeling, it would be closer to the time Rinpoche and Yeshi left.

"When will that be?" I asked, trying to keep the little tremble of emotion out of my voice. "When will his teacher be coming to Tangyeling?"

"Oh, but he's already here," Dr. Bell said.

I looked up, confused.

"In all the excitement, I completely forgot my manners," Dr. Bell said, turning to face Yeshi with his palms pressed together to make prayer hands, his head bowing low.

"Welcome home, Rinpoche-la."

Yeshi's eyes met mine, and his expression was mischievous. I waited for him to laugh and correct Dr. Bell. But he didn't. Yeshi made prayer hands too and smiled at Dr. Bell.

"Thank you," Yeshi said. "I am very glad to be back."

I stared at Yeshi, my mouth hanging open in amazement.

"You?" I asked, utterly incredulous.

"Me," he said. "I was three years old when a search party came to my village. Two monks wearing ordinary clothes. They had toys, little wind-up trucks and rubber balls and balloons — my brothers were fascinated with them. But the only thing I wanted was the man's *mala* — his prayer beads. Every time he tried to take them back, he said I shouted, 'No, these are mine,' and swatted his hand away. The monk was very interested in this, because the *mala* had actually belonged to Lokesh Rinpoche — he was my Lama Jampa Rinpoche's teacher. After that, more monks came and they did many tests, showed me other things and asked which ones were mine. I picked out a walking stick, a pair of glasses, and a small bell. They had all been Lokesh Rinpoche's during his lifetime.

"So they brought me to Lama Jampa. Because Lama Jampa was Lokesh Rinpoche's student for so many years, they thought he would know best if they had found the correct child. This part I remember — the first thing I did when I saw him was to shout, 'Dawa-la!' This was a nickname Lokesh Rinpoche had for Lama Jampa. He knew at that moment he had found me, that his teacher, Lokesh Rinpoche, had returned."

I watched him gather up some stray pieces of onion peel and neatly sweep them into one hand. He tossed the peelings into the garbage can. *Yeshi is a* tulku, I thought, staring at him. A brilliant and important teacher who has returned to live again to continue his work. Here I thought he was just a kid like me. In addition to being in a total state of shock, I also felt embarrassed. I would have been so much more . . . careful, more respectful or whatever, if only I'd known.

"But . . . why didn't you tell me?" I asked.

Dr. Bell stood up. "If the two of you don't mind, I'm going to step outside and give the police another ring, see if they're on their way yet. I'll be back shortly."

I nodded, then looked back at Yeshi. He looked very serious.

"I think yes, I should have told you," Yeshi said. "But I was selfish."

"Selfish?" I asked.

He nodded. "I came to live in Jampa Rinpoche's monastery when I was five. When you are identified as the reincarnation of a teacher, there is much work to do, much studying. So much to learn. I loved living at Samye. Jampa Rinpoche was like my own family. It was my path, and I wanted to be there. But there was one thing I did not like. I could not make any friends."

"There were no other children at the monastery?" I asked.

"There were many children, many boys also studying to be young monks. In Tibet it is an honor for a family to send one son to a monastery. Every family that can send a son does. So there were many boys my own age. But they all knew I was a *tulku*. They knew I was a teacher returning to them. I felt I was just an ordinary monk. But the boys did not treat me that way. They were polite and very respectful. But they were not friends. I felt they were my equals, ordinary monks just like me. But they did not think so. They could not be themselves with me. And so I never made a real friend."

I shook my head. "I'm so sorry, Yeshi. That must have been really hard."

He smiled. "Yes, but then finally Jampa Rinpoche said it was time for us to go to America to Tangyeling, which would one day become mine. And so we came. And then I looked outside, and you were standing there, watching Rinpoche throat sing. And as soon as I started talking to you, I knew I wanted us to be friends. I wanted you to think I was just ordinary. And it worked, yes? Because we *are* friends."

I gave him a huge smile. "Yes, we are," I said.

"But it was wrong of me to keep it from you," Yeshi said.

"Actually, no. I think if I had known or understood who you were, that all of this was for you, I might not have felt so relaxed around you. I would have been too intimidated. I'm glad you didn't tell me. And I'm glad I know now!"

Yeshi laughed. "But nothing is different. I'm a simple, ordinary monk, okay?"

I nodded. "Okay. Did your family go with you to the monastery?"

"Oh, no," Yeshi said. "They were farmers. They needed to work. And they needed to care for my brothers and sisters."

"So you didn't see them?"

"A few times, you know. For ceremonies and things, they would come. But otherwise, no."

"But that must have been so hard. You must have missed them so much."

"Yes," Yeshi said. "But I was going to a family too — all the monks and teachers. When you are Rinpoche, you are brother and son and father to everyone. And, one day, teacher to everyone. And this made me happy. And it made my mother and father happy."

"Wow," I said. "I can't imagine only seeing my parents a few times a year. Though with the way my mom and I have been fighting, it's amazing I'd feel that way."

"Why do you fight?" Yeshi asked.

I sighed, and told him about Kizzy's close call, and how things had been since then. And how it had all exploded earlier in the day, because we had gone looking for the rainbow.

"I realize now how scared she was today. How scared she is all the time. And I blew it. I know I deserve to be punished for that. But part of that punishment is not letting me come back here. Which was already the worst thing ever, but now that I know you're staying, I don't know what to do. I did really mess up today, but not enough to deserve never being allowed to see you again. But she's already said that's the way it's going to be. It makes me so angry."

Yeshi pulled the bowl of momo ingredients from me and gave it a few stirs. His face looked thoughtful. After a while, he pushed the bowl aside and looked at me.

"It must be very, very hard to live that way. I feel great compassion for anyone in that situation."

"It is hard," I said. "I feel like I'm in prison."

"I didn't mean you," Yeshi said gently. "I meant your mother. She's stuck in a cycle that started when your sister almost drowned. That experience made her very scared, and no one likes to feel fear. So she is trying to avoid feeling more fear by keeping your sister safe, and the only way she can do that is to be afraid of everything she imagines might harm your sister. There is no time for her to enjoy the present moment, to be happy, because she is a prisoner of fear. She is trapped in a circle of suffering."

I blinked back the tears in my eyes. I felt moved and a little ashamed to hear him talk about my mother with such compassion. He didn't even know her. Why hadn't I understood her better? Probably because I was so worried about my own feelings, I'd completely forgotten to think about hers.

"But how does a person avoid suffering?" I asked.

"It's a good question, and the answer is strange," he told me. "You avoid suffering by knowing you cannot avoid suffering. By accepting that it is a part of life, and that it comes to us all."

"I don't get it," I said.

"You could attend teachings all your life and maybe still not get it," Yeshi said. "But I think really what it means is we will make friends, and some of them will go away. We will have nice things but lose or break them. We will love people, and some of them will leave us. We are healthy, but sometimes we might get sick. It is very hard for us to live like that, trying to avoid losing the people and things we love. So we get really attached to not letting that happen. And of course we can be safe and smart and sensible, but we can't control everything. Nobody can."

Yeshi got up and fetched the round dough wrappers he'd made earlier that day, along with two spoons. He handed me one.

"Do what I do," he said. "You can't mess it up."

He placed a spoonful of the mixed ingredients in the center of the dough, then twisted it into a neat dumpling.

"You try," he said. "So all I'm really saying is, when someone is okay with the fact that living means both good things and bad things will happen but we can still be happy, no matter what — that is escaping suffering. Someone who is okay with that can live in the present and enjoy life, not waste time worrying about next week, or next year. A person like your mother, who is scared all the time that one day she might be scared again of something that might never happen — she is suffering. But people can learn to change that."

"Even my mom?" I asked.

"Of course even your mom," he replied. "That's right, now just press the ends of the dough together, like you're making a little present. Make sure every end is sealed to another end, or the insides will fall out of the dumpling."

"But how would I ever get her to understand that?" I asked, trying to imitate what he had done with the dough wrapper. "I'm not a teacher like you — I totally understand it when you explain it, but I could never explain it so she'd really get it. I can't do what you do, Yeshi."

"Are you sure?" he said, with a mischievous smile. He plucked the momo I'd been struggling with off the plate, placed it next to the momo he'd made, then spun the plate around. And there were two identical, perfect momos. As hard as I stared at them, I couldn't tell which one was Yeshi's, and which one was mine.

"Just imagine," Yeshi said as he handed me another dough wrapper, "what other things you could do, if you stopped worrying about failing and just tried."

Chapter Fifteen

"Would it be okay if I talked first?" I asked.

My parents were sitting on the living room couch, both of them wearing the expression of shocked amazement they'd had since a police SUV delivered me to my front door a half hour earlier.

My father glanced at my mother, who said nothing.

"Sure," he told me.

"Okay. First, I want you to know I'm not going to try to minimize what I did today. I know how serious it is, and I'm not trying to excuse my behavior. There are some things I want to explain to kind of give you a fuller picture of what happened, but I'm only doing that so you'll know what went on today. I'm not trying to defend myself."

My mother remained silent. My father nodded at me to go on.

"I disobeyed Mom twice today. The first time was sheer stupidity. Mom was very clear — do not go outside the house for any reason. But because there was something out there Kizzy wanted to see, I decided that it would be okay to go just a little bit outside, for just a short time. I thought Mom was being unfair making us stay inside. But I realize now it didn't matter what I thought. It'd be like getting pulled over for speeding and telling the cop the speed limit was too slow so you ignored it and shouldn't get a ticket. Breaking a rule is breaking a rule. I get that now."

My father gave me a small, encouraging smile. My mother still said nothing, but she was looking at me now.

"Second, I want to apologize to Mom for what she went through this morning because of me. It obviously brought back what happened last summer. Not only were we gone, but we were at the one place she was the most scared of — the creek. That must have been terrible for you, Mom, to relive being scared like that again. I'm really sorry I did that to you."

My mother rubbed her hand across her forehead, then met my gaze again.

"Thank you," she said softly.

"Okay. So third. I reacted way too strongly when you grounded me. You had a good reason for doing it. And I was mad. I've been mad for a long time about all the rules and restrictions and stuff, but that's another subject. But today in particular, I truly believed it was important for me to get to the monastery. I believed it was maybe the most important thing I've ever had to do. And I still believe that."

"Why?" my mother asked. "Because that is something I simply don't understand. Why you would head out there when you were grounded, when you were already in trouble? When there was a bad storm coming?"

I nodded. "I can't explain it all right now, not the background. I want to tell you about Yeshi and Rinpoche, and why I think they're so amazing, and how being around them has changed me. And I will tell you. But the reason I had to get up there today was because I thought they were in danger."

"In danger?" my mother asked, sitting up very straight. "Because of the attempted theft that the policeman was talking about when he dropped you off?"

Yeah, it wasn't the greatest tactic to throw that detail in, I knew. Now it was clear that it was no mistake I'd been at the monastery when the almost-theft took place. But I had to be honest now. I still knew barely enough about Buddhism to cover my little finger, but I knew that truthfulness was important.

"Yes," I said. I told them about the statue, and about the Ocean Walker, and how I'd needed to warn Yeshi and Rinpoche about him.

"Wait, wait, wait," my father said. "How would you know what this black-market art dealer looked like? Or when he planned to hit the monastery?"

"Because he came to our house," I said. "That guy claiming to be a DEP agent. It's complicated, but I just had a feeling. And he was poking around here again and I confronted him with what I suspected, and after that, I was sure he was going to the monastery to do whatever he had to to get his hands on that statue."

"What? When was he poking around here? Why didn't you tell us?" my mother asked.

"Or call the police?" my father added.

"And tell them what? That I thought a guy might be planning on robbing a monastery of an ancient relic? Nothing had happened yet. And I didn't know the guy's name or where he was or anything. At that point, there was nothing to report!"

"True," my father said. "But you could have told us."

"I know," I agreed. "But I knew I had to get up to the monastery as fast as I could to warn them. They don't have a phone; there's no paved road up there. Mom was already furious at me, and even if she hadn't been, my story would have sounded pretty crazy. I had to get up there myself. There was no other way to warn them. And I was right."

"This art dealer — the police said he forced his way into the monastery," my father said.

I nodded. "Him and another guy. And they threatened to hurt Rinpoche. The Ocean Walker made —"

"The Ocean Walker?" my mother asked, shaking her head in confusion.

"Sorry, I mean the art dealer guy. He made Yeshi and me go into this basement storage room where he thought the statue was hidden. And he said if I didn't help him find it, Rinpoche was going to get hurt. So I helped him find it."

"But if it had been hidden all that time, how would you have known where to look?" my mother asked.

"Well, I'd kind of been studying this old text, a kind of prophecy, looking for clues," I said.

"You've been studying old Buddhist texts," my father repeated. I nodded and he burst out laughing.

"Sorry, that's just not something I ever expected to hear you say," he said. "Go on."

I explained everything, about the Ocean Walker finding the statue, and Dr. Bell showing up and helping us escape him and save Rinpoche. And about Mo-Mo chasing the Ocean Walker down the mountain and not coming back.

"I'm not trying to get out of being in trouble," I said when I finished. "I just wanted to explain, because I never would have done what I did if I didn't feel it was more important than anything — I was afraid for Yeshi and Rinpoche. That they might get hurt."

"With good reason, I'd say," my father told me.

The phone rang. My father got up and went into the kitchen to answer it.

"I really am sorry," I told my mother. "Whatever you decide, whatever you think my punishment should be, I'll accept it, and I won't fight with you or give you attitude or anything."

"All right," she said. "Look, Jackson, I'm still kind of reeling from everything that happened today. But I want you to know that I truly appreciate what you said to me just now. And I also want you to know that I'm starting to understand the effect of . . . how my reaction to what happened to Kizzy has affected you. It changed me. I know that. I never thought I'd be this kind of mother, controlling and suspicious of everything. I only wanted to keep both of you safe, but what I accomplished was to make you hate me."

"I don't hate you!" I exclaimed, getting out of my chair and moving to the couch where my mother was sitting. I sat next to her and put my arms around her. "I don't hate you. I love you."

She hugged me back. "I love you too," she whispered. "And I'm sorry for being so anxious all the time. I'm sorry for keeping you on such a tight leash. Honestly, I thought I would feel better, more relaxed, as time went by. But I don't. And I don't know what to do about that. I don't think there's anything I *can* do."

I sat back and looked at her, hesitating. I wasn't sure this was the right time to start being a cheerleader for

Yeshi and Rinpoche and the teachings they had to offer. But Yeshi had told me I shouldn't worry about failing.

"There are things you can do, Mom," I said.

She sat back on the couch and looked at me.

"Okay, again, I know I'm grounded until the end of time and everything. This isn't about that. But while I've been spending time with Yeshi, he's told me a little about what Buddhism is, how it can help people, especially when they're having trouble with worrying."

"How?"

I took a deep breath.

"It was a terrible scare, maybe the worst one of your life, when Kizzy almost drowned," I began.

She nodded.

"And since then, you've gotten — no offense — kind of obsessed with keeping Kizzy away from situations where she might get hurt, because you don't ever want to feel scared like that again."

My mother nodded. "That's right."

"Okay. So Yeshi says a big part of Buddhism is knowing that as much as you never want to get in an accident, or get a yucky disease, or lose something really important to you, there's really no way you can ever guarantee those things won't happen. We fall down. We get stomach viruses."

"Yes, that's true," she agreed.

"So because we're so scared of getting a disease, we spend lots of every day trying to avoid it. Every time we go to a party or a movie or a bookstore, all we can think about is the germs everywhere and how we can't get too close to anyone or touch anything they've touched or eat any food someone might have breathed on."

"Okay," she said. "I'm following you."

"No matter what, we could get sick anyway. But in the meantime, we go out and do all those things, but we never have fun because we're so focused on not getting anybody's germs."

"Right."

"We want to avoid getting sick because being sick doesn't feel good, but we end up not feeling good even doing things that should be fun. We miss feeling good because we're too busy trying to avoid feeling bad. So we, like, waste parts of our lives because we're worrying about something nobody can control."

"Hmm. I never thought about it that way. But even if that's true, I'm not going to ever stop being careful. I'm a parent — that's what parents do."

"I know," I said. "But there are things you can learn, about noticing when your brain is kind of taking over and making you scared — Yeshi told me that you can learn to stop that sometimes and remember to just enjoy whatever is happening at the moment."

"Yeshi explained all that to you?" she asked.

I nodded. "He's really smart," I said. "He's been learn-ing about Buddhism all his life — he's going to be a monk and a teacher."

Definitely best to leave out the whole reincarnation thing for the time being. Maybe one day, Mom would be ready to hear about demons and *tulkus*. But today was not that day.

"He sounds like a pretty special kid," she said, taking my chin in her hand and turning my face toward hers.

"He is," I said, tears springing into my eyes. "He's, like, my best friend ever."

She looked at me thoughtfully for a moment, then nodded.

"You know, I've seen some of the worst behavior you've ever displayed all in one day — this day," she said.

I looked down.

"I know," I murmured.

"Now that everybody's had a chance to cool down, I'll talk to your dad about what happened, and what the consequences should be."

"I know," I said, still looking down.

"But everything you've said to me and your dad since you got home tonight has also been very different from anything I've seen before from you. You've been forth-right, you've taken responsibility for your actions, and you've actually given me some very good advice. I can see how maybe this Yeshi might be a good influence on you."

I looked up at her, a sliver of hope creeping into my heart.

"I don't like what you did, running up to the monastery today. But I like *why* you did it. And Yeshi and his teacher obviously mean a great deal to you. I also don't like that I've treated you unfairly more than I'd like to think, this last year. So whatever your father and I decide, Jax, I want you to know I'm not going to forbid you to go up there, or to see your friend."

I gasped and threw my arms around my mother.

"Oh, Mom, thank you. Thank you so much!"

"Hey, this looks happy," I heard my father say as he returned to the living room.

I pulled away from my mother and looked at him.

"I'm still allowed to see Yeshi," I said, beaming.

"Well, I'm glad to hear it," my dad said. "Glad for both of you. And we won't need to worry about your being on the mountain either. That was the police on the phone. They caught both of the men — the art dealer and his helper. Right now they're thinking the accomplice, Walter Ogden they said his name is, had no idea what he was getting into. He got paid a hundred bucks to basically be intimidating. But this other guy, Everett Ravenwood — apparently, there is a whole bunch of people very interested in having him apprehended. He's stolen a lot of artifacts from a lot of people. And now he's also violated federal law by impersonating a DEP officer.

So I don't think we need to worry about seeing him back on the mountain the next decade or so."

"Where was he? Where did they find him?" I asked eagerly.

"He'd gotten himself lost in the woods on the mountain," my father said, chuckling. "Apparently, he wasn't that hard to find."

I stood up.

"And Mo-Mo? Did they find Mo-Mo?"

"The dog?" my father asked. "No, not that they mentioned. Why?"

I sat back down again, my heart heavy.

"I told you Mo-Mo chased the guy, Ravenwood, out of the monastery. When he didn't come back, Yeshi and I figured he was going to follow the man, make sure he didn't return to hurt us, or anybody. I thought when they found the Oce — when they found Ravenwood, they'd find Mo-Mo too."

"I'm sorry, sweetie. There was no dog with the guy. They said he was all alone."

I wiped a tear from my eye.

"Oh, Jackson, try not to worry," my mother said. "He is a huge, strong dog. I'm sure he can take care of himself. There's nothing in those woods that can hurt him. And he's obviously very intelligent. I know it's upsetting, but I'm sure Mo-Mo will find his way home."

I looked at my mother in surprise. It was the first time

she'd referred to him as anything but "that animal" —
the first time she'd called him by his name.

"Thanks, Mom," I said, my voice wavering.

"Hey, maybe he went back to the monastery," she said
suddenly. "That would make sense, right? If the weather's clear in the morning, you could go up and check, see
if he went there. Would that make you feel better?"

I stared at my mother, amazed. I nodded.

"Really? You'd really let me do that?" I asked.

"Just to check for Mo-Mo," she said. "And to check
on your friends. You're still grounded. But now that I
know the police have locked those two guys up, then
yes, you can go up there to look for Mo-Mo. I trust you."

Chapter Sixteen

The sky was so clear and the sun so brilliant, it was hard to imagine there had been such a storm. The only clue was the many branches that had come down in the heavy winds. Yeshi had brought out a large blanket and spread it on the damp grass beneath the prayer flags. We sat facing each other. The mountain was completely quiet except for the whisper of the wind in the trees. Yeshi was not dressed in jeans and a T-shirt today. He was wearing maroon robes like Rinpoche's. When I looked at his face, he looked like regular old Yeshi. But every time he adjusted his robes, he looked like a different person. Older. A little more intense. Then he'd look at me, or smile, and he'd be Yeshi again. It was going to take some getting used to.

"I just hoped so much that I'd find him here," I said to Yeshi, probably for the third time.

"I know."

"I wish I could at least know that he's okay," I said, looking hopefully at Yeshi. I wanted him to tell me something magical and optimistic, that Mo-Mo had helped save Rinpoche and therefore he could come to no harm. Something.

"It's hard to not know," Yeshi agreed.

"What do you think I should do?" I asked.

"I don't think you should do anything," Yeshi said. "I think you should let time do the work for you. Try to keep your mind settled, and away from thinking about the outcome. Whatever happens to Mo-Mo has to be okay in your heart."

I nodded glumly.

"It isn't easy for me to do that," I said. "I'm not a Buddhist."

Yeshi shrugged.

"Being a Buddhist doesn't mean you don't worry about stuff, or that you never get really sad or crazy about something. But if you're a Buddhist, then you learn to notice when you are worrying too much, when you're thinking too much. And you send the thoughts away — you turn them into little clouds, and a puff of wind makes them float off. And when the worrying thoughts come back, you send them away again. That's what a Buddhist does. The point isn't to never ever worry or have bad thoughts. The point is to keep remembering to shoo the thoughts away when you notice them."

"I'll have to remember to tell my mom that," I said. "I think she kind of understood about how trying to avoid feeling bad just ends up making you feel bad. And she said I could come back here today, to look for Mo-Mo."

"You talked to her with no fighting!" Yeshi exclaimed happily.

"I did," I said with a grin. "Because of you. And I have amazing news: The police caught the Ocean Walker! They caught his helper too. So you and Rinpoche don't need to be worried about that."

"We're very grateful," Yeshi said, making a small tower of mani stones by balancing one on top of another. "And thank you for explaining that in this country we don't need to be afraid of the police."

"Yeah," I said. "They're the good guys here. You should never be afraid of them. I have to say, though, I have never been so scared in my life as I was when I heard the sounds of horses' hooves last night. Although now I'm starting to think maybe my mind was just playing a trick on me."

"I heard them too," Yeshi said, his eyes focused on his balancing act.

"You did? So it was really Tsiu Marpo? And the six demon riders?"

"Maybe."

"And you don't find that at all scary?" I pressed.

"A demon? Of course I do," he replied matter-of-factly.

"You don't sound scared."

Yeshi shrugged. "That was yesterday. It isn't happening today."

He had a point. I picked up a mani stone and gingerly added it to his pile.

"Rinpoche was amazing. Even when that guy grabbed him and made like he was going to hit him with the club, Rinpoche looked so . . . serene. Like he looks when he's meditating. It's as if he knew that nothing bad was going to happen to him."

"That's not quite it," Yeshi said. "Rinpoche knows that something bad can happen to him, at any time. It's just as I explained to you, but Rinpoche has been studying the teachings all his life, and he is very old. He accepts that he has no control over what might occur. That gives him the space he needs to be peaceful and present in every single moment."

"I wish I could study those teachings," I said, with a small laugh.

"You can," Yeshi said. "Anyone can. One of the things we will do here is offer classes, once more monks have come. Anyone will be able to come and learn, if they want."

"I'd love to do that," I said. "Maybe my mom would come too! So there are other monks coming?"

Yeshi nodded. "I will have more teachers, and others will live and study here after Rinpoche has left."

"Will Rinpoche be leaving soon?" I asked.

Yeshi's expression darkened, his eyes sad.

"Yes," he said. "Very soon."

"How long will it be before you'll see him again?"

Yeshi's hand closed over a mani stone.

"I will never see Rinpoche again," he said quietly.

I sat up very straight. "Wait, what do you mean? I know Tibet is really far away, but that doesn't mean you can't ever go back there."

Yeshi sighed. "Unless many things change, Jax, I actually cannot ever go back to Tibet. And once Rinpoche returns, they will probably not let him leave again, not after he left without permission to go to America."

I stared at my friend. "I don't get it. Why? Who's 'they'?"

Yeshi chewed on his lower lip for a moment. "A Tibetan cannot leave Tibet or enter Tibet without permission from the government," he explained. "We almost certainly would not have been given permission to leave and travel to America, so we sneaked out. We went over the Himalayas. Rinpoche will be able to sneak back in; there are many waiting to help him. But the government may know he has been missing, and it will be too dangerous for him to ever try leaving again. They will be watching him now. They will think he is a spy."

"But why would the Tibetan government be dangerous to Rinpoche? To any monk?"

"The government isn't Tibetan, Jax. It's Chinese. Chinese armies came to Tibet many years ago, in 1950. The soldiers killed many people, and made Tibet part of China. Most of our monasteries were destroyed. Many of our traditions were outlawed. It is very hard to be Tibetan in Tibet now. That is why Tangyeling was built in America. We had to rebuild the most important monasteries in other countries, like India and Nepal. And now America. The only way to keep our teachings and our culture alive now is to do it outside of Tibet."

"Then why is Rinpoche going back?" I asked.

"Because his monastery is still there. And he refuses to give up living the old ways in his own country. Even if he risks ending up in prison by doing so."

"Prison? It's that bad?" I asked.

"In Tibet now, it's far worse than you can possibly imagine," Yeshi said quietly. "That is why I can't go back. Now that I am recognized as a *tulku*, I am one of those people who will spend the rest of my life keeping our teachings alive in the traditional Tibetan way. The government does not like that. So I cannot risk going back until the government stops punishing us for keeping the old ways alive, or until Tibet becomes free again."

"But that's crazy!" I exclaimed. "You must really hate the Chinese."

"I don't hate anyone," Yeshi said. "And certainly not my Chinese brothers and sisters. It is not Chinese people who have done this, Jax. It is a government, it is armies — the Chinese Communist Party. It is a small group of people with a huge amount of power who will do anything to keep their power. The CCP has hurt as many Chinese people as it has Tibetans. I feel love and compassion for the citizens of China. But the government, the military, it is harder for me to feel compassion for them."

I tried not to stare at him. I thought about how I would feel if I had to go to a country halfway around the world and leave Mom and Dad and Kizzy behind. I couldn't take it, I thought. I'd be a mess, sobbing all the time. How did Yeshi get to be so strong?

Neither of us said anything for a long time. Orange- and rose-colored light shimmered across the grass as the sun moved higher in the sky.

"I'm going to need to go soon," I said reluctantly. "I promised my mom I'd be home after checking on you and Rinpoche and seeing if Mo-Mo was here."

"Yes," Yeshi said, putting the mani stones down and getting to his feet. "And I will have chores and studying. And Dr. Bell will be returning to visit Rinpoche tomorrow, so I will need to get things ready for him."

I got up too, watching Yeshi as he adjusted his robe and threw one corner over his left shoulder, just the way Rinpoche did.

"Um, I'm supposed to call you Rinpoche now, right?" I asked.

Yeshi rolled his eyes.

"Enough people will be calling me Rinpoche," he said. "Please keep calling me Yeshi."

I nodded. "Okay. But hey, I mean . . . congratulations and everything."

"Thanks," he said.

But even though Yeshi was still Yeshi, I knew things had changed at the monastery. He would be studying more, meditating more, doing more. He wore robes now. Other monks would come to live there too. It would be the same, but not quite the same.

"Are you coming back tomorrow?" Yeshi asked.

"Oh! I mean yes, if that's okay," I said, jumbling the words as I tried to get them out too quickly. "And if my mom lets me. I thought maybe we needed to be more . . . formal now, or something."

"Me, formal?" Yeshi asked, laughing. "Nah. Always come. This is your monastery too, Jax. I want you to treat it like your home."

A big smile crossed my face, the kind you can't really control and worry might make you look a little crazy.

"Okay, thanks," I said. "So I'll be back tomorrow if I can. But if not, don't worry. I'll be back eventually. Maybe I'll even bring you a cell phone!"

"Dr. Bell left his with Rinpoche," Yeshi said with a grin. "Oh, and I found this when I was sweeping out the shrine room this morning. It was under one of the meditation cushions."

He handed me my cell phone, which I took gratefully. At least my parents wouldn't have to worry about replacing it.

"Bye," I said.

"Until soon," Yeshi said.

Yeshi strode across the lawn, his robe brushing the tips of the grass. He looked like he'd grown a few inches, but maybe it was just the way he moved so confidently, as though he'd been walking over the grass to Tangyeling's front door all his life.

I walked in the opposite direction — not toward the logging road where the police had driven their big SUV, but my old way, to Lotus Trail. As I walked, I thought about what Yeshi had told me, about how difficult it was to be Tibetan in Tibet. How he could never go back, and Rinpoche could never leave. I thought of his family and how it must have hurt them to give him up, let him go to America so he could do his part to keep the teachings alive.

What did it feel like to have to give up your family? Give up your country? It was impossible for me to even begin to imagine. I wasn't strong like they were. I still had to fight back tears when I thought about Mo-Mo and the way he'd disappeared so abruptly. Yeshi had told me that Rinpoche was peaceful because he was able to accept change, and good and bad things happening. But I wasn't like that. Rinpoche was leaving. Yeshi was staying, but he would have more lessons, more teachers, perhaps classes to teach himself. And Mo-Mo wasn't at the monastery. He was gone. And in my heart, I no longer held much hope that he was coming back.

I knew that Mo-Mo's magical appearance in my life wasn't about me. It was about fulfilling a prophecy, and protecting something sacred that belonged in Tibet. Mo-Mo didn't come into my life to make me happy, to keep me company, to make me feel safe and special the way he never left my side and seemed to read my thoughts. But he had done all those things anyway. I was no longer convinced that Mo-Mo was lost on the mountain. He had done what he was meant to do, acted as protector so the statue of Tsiu Marpo could be saved. It made sense to me that, having fulfilled his role, he would disappear as magically as he had appeared in the first place.

But that didn't make me feel peaceful. It made me feel miserable. Was he ever real at all? Or was he more phantom than anything else, something like Tsiu Marpo, that could seem like it was there but wasn't? No, I told myself. Mo-Mo was real. I needed to believe in him. When he was with me, Mo-Mo was no ghost — he was my dog, my friend, and my protector. I believed in him because he had believed in me. I owed him that much.

I walked cautiously down the steeper, rockier part of the path, being careful not to lose my footing in the stones and dirt that had been loosened by the heavy rain. I reached the flatter place where the path widened and approached the road, and I began to pick up my pace when suddenly something in the brush to the side of the trail caught my eye. I bent down to get a better look at it, and exclaimed with surprise. It was a mani stone, a large, brightly colored one.

"Where did that come from?" I said out loud. I picked it up and examined it. It didn't look like the ones Yeshi painted. The paint seemed different, the colors deeper, and the lettering was raised, as if it had been carved out of the rock first, then painted. It was absolutely beautiful. I started to lean down to put it back, when I heard something rustle behind me, and I froze. Still holding the stone, I straightened my back, and very slowly I turned around to face whatever had just stepped onto the trail behind me.

It was a dog.

"Mo-Mo!" I yelled, dropping the stone and falling to my knees. I wrapped my arms around his massive neck and buried my face in his lion's mane. I hugged him as tightly as I could, saying his name over and over again, my voice muffled in his coat.

"Are you okay, boy? Are you hurt?" I asked, when I finally drew back to look at him.

He gazed back at me solemnly. He looked as perfect as he had the first day I saw him. His coat was shiny and looked freshly brushed. His paws were clean and his eyes were bright — he looked like he'd just come from the Westminster dog show.

"You came back," I whispered, my eyes filling with tears. "Will you stay this time, Mo-Mo? We'll go up to the monastery whenever we can. I'll take care of you, and we can both take care of Yeshi. And Kizzy. We need you, Mo-Mo. I love you, boy. You'll stay, won't you? For good this time?"

Mo-Mo stood up and trotted down the path toward the road, then looped back and walked toward me, his tail wagging.

I laughed out loud. I could kind of read Mo-Mo's mind too, at least sometimes. Like right now. I knew exactly what he was telling me. He was saying, *Yes, I will stay with you.* And he was saying, *Yes, you will take care of me, and I will also take care of you.*

My heart suddenly felt as light and powerful as a prayer flag. Mo-Mo waited until I caught up with him, then walked at my side. But when we reached the road, he darted ahead again, looped back, darted ahead another time, and I knew he was as eager as I was to get where we were going.

Home.

Author's note

Grateful thanks and acknowledgment to Christopher Bell, whose extensive firsthand knowledge of all things Tibetan from the linguistic to the demonic was instrumental in my writing.

I will be donating a portion of the proceeds I receive from this book to TibetAid, an international relief organization dedicated to providing humanitarian assistance to Tibetans in Tibet as well as those living in exile. The organization's vision is to see Tibetan culture, traditions, and religions remain alive and flourishing. For more information on TibetAid's programs, including individual sponsorships and medical and educational programs, please visit www.tibetaid.org.